Into the Ruins

Issue 9
Spring 2018

Published May 2018 by Figuration Press
Portland, Oregon

Into the Ruins is a project and publication of Figuration Press,
a small publication house focused on alternate visions of the future
and alternate ways of understanding the world,
particularly in ecological contexts.

intotheruins.com

figurationpress.com

ISBN 13: 978-0-9978656-7-7
ISBN 10: 0-9978656-7-9

Editor's Note:
With a certain melancholy for the state of the world,
which is too often too hard to keep away.

Comments and feedback always welcome at editor@intotheruins.com
Comments for authors will be forwarded.

Issue 9
Spring 2018

TABLE OF CONTENTS

PREAMBLE

STORIES

PREAMBLE

THE GENERALIST
BY JOEL CARIS

I CELEBRATED THE BEGINNING OF MAY by weeding carrots and planting onions. I did not do this in my own backyard, in my own garden, but at a farm near the coast run by two good friends, giving them one of the days of my life in exchange for the sustenance of pointed digging in the dirt. I helped weed two hundred bed feet of baby carrots by hand (a tedious task that I have somehow always enjoyed) and helped lay out and then plant a couple thousand onion starts. By the end of the day (really, by the middle of the day), my back hurt, my legs were sore, I was hot and sweaty, and it all felt delightful. The dirt and vegetables reminded me how out of shape I was, but these small acts of farming came back easily—familiar rituals giving me so much. I left the farm with a giant bag of fresh arugula and a familiar sense of satisfaction.

It was one day; after a Grange meeting that evening, I drove back to Portland and came home to my wife, Kate. This was a familiar ritual, too, giving me just as much, and bringing back a sense of wholeness I always lose the nights I sleep alone out on the coast or when Kate leaves town for a work trip, as she did the next morning. In the morning, I awoke in the city; I took the bus downtown to attend a training, sitting in a room of professionals and discussing the sort of topics urban professionals sometimes do, most but not all of the dirt out from under my chewed nails. Afterwards I came home, texted with my wife, ran two loads of laundry and hung them in our backyard to dry, watered the garden, and continued to work on putting together the issue of *Into the Ruins* you now hold in your hands.

I still felt sore, the act of growing food echoing in my muscles. I missed Kate. I made a dinner of potatoes and asparagus from the farmers market, a simple salad fresh with the arugula I brought home the day before, and a lamb leg steak from the freezer, perhaps (amazingly) four years old now, from a lamb I almost certainly helped to raise years back at the exact same place I had been the day before weeding carrots and planting onions: the past echoing into the present, my future promising further calls to my past even as it unfolds into something new, a complex origami of everything that has come before.

How does all this piece together, how did that plate of food come to be tied together over years of work? My friends are farming on land that is part of a ranch I used to work on at the coast. In 2012, we lived there together for a summer, in the ranch's old farm house, brought together by a vegetable operation just down the road we had both worked for. It's a complicated story, really, but also simple: we came to the same place to farm vegetables, a year apart, and all of us ended up sharing a house on a ranch, helping to tend animals for our rent, growing vegetables and canning food and drinking and listening to music and engaging in long conversations and reveling in the summer sun and piecing it all together in a rural area, young and groping our way toward some kind of coherent life. After that summer, we went our own ways; they moved, I stayed, and we continued to seek out a life that made sense, that somehow pulled together so many disparate threads and desires into a functional whole.

Then they returned and I left, moving to Portland to live with Kate but still making twice monthly trips to the coast for work. Eventually, my friends found their way back to that same ranch, but this time with the intention of farming a stretch of its deep and beautiful soil. That's where they are today and where I was last week, digging in the dirt, helping in those small, early rituals that will bring forth food from the ground. That's where the arugula salad I ate for dinner came from, dressed and slightly wilted next to a piece of lamb that had come from the same place, only years earlier. Everything came together on that plate—a small explication of a small slice of shared history. Food does this. It's one of many reasons I return to it over and over again.

How many different kinds of lives did I live in those two days? Farming, my marriage, my day job, this magazine, even my role at the Grange: all of them and more in about thirty-six hours. I was in the city and the country, getting dirty and sitting in a conference room surrounded by well-dressed professionals while listening to an expert. I walked, rode the bus, rode light rail, and drove a car. How many different types of people did I interact with? How many world views, political opinions, types of lives lived did I brush up against? Even by my standards it was an impressive two days.

Still, in a matter of kind if not degree, this isn't unique for me. One thing I have learned about myself over the years is that I am a generalist, despite the fact that I love to get bogged down in details. There are pros and cons to this strategy. I like taking the time and opportunity to explore many ways of living and many of the subjects that interest me. However, I also often over-stretch myself, sometimes fail to master subjects I would like to, and am too quick to become interested in and commit to something only to move on once it proves more difficult than I expected —or when I just find something else to become *more* interested in. (Anyone who has followed my blogging adventures may be nodding their head in agreement.)

That said, there's a joy in being a generalist—at least, for me there is. The world is large and full of fascinating people, places, subjects, and opportunities, and I do not want to close too many of them off to myself. Still, there's another piece to this, and it's related to this magazine's philosophy. Considered in the context of a challenging future defined by natural limits, the need for generalists is likely to be higher than today. An economy that is decentralizing and simplifying is likely to shed a good deal of specialists and to cast about for a good deal more generalists. In such a future, being a generalist may very well be an excellent adaptation. After all, the ability to run a household economy with limited resources is a very good skill set to have in hard times, and it's a skill set made up of the ability to perform a wide variety of tasks with a basic level of proficiency. It's the shunning of special-ization—of a very developed skill in one particular area—for the ability to do a wide variety of things well enough; to, in other words, make do.

There's more to it than just that, though. In my experience, being a generalist and having a wide variety of skills, a wide variety of experiences, and a wide variety of acquaintances makes it a lot easier to deal with an unexpected future. If there is one very definite defining feature I expect the future to hold, it's one of disruption and newfound variability. Our current ways of doing things are already going hay-wire in unexpected ways, and I see no reason to believe that trend line is going to re-verse itself. The future is *not* going to look like the past (even if it may feature some lovely revivals of past technologies well-adapted to low-energy contexts) and those who are able to adapt and change—or who are familiar enough with different ways of living and being so as to slip comfortably from one to the other as outside influ-ences dictate—are likely to have a much easier go of things than those who rigidly define their lives and are unable to change as needed.

To my mind, this is one of the greatest advantages of being a generalist: I think I'm relatively adept at rolling with the punches, so to speak. I have made my living on less than a thousand dollars a month, and I've made it on a few multiples more. I've lived alone and lived in communal situations. I've lived in rural areas and cities; lived a professional life and a working class one; can work a spreadsheet and a plot of land; don't too terribly mind being covered in animal manure and still am capable of dressing up in nice clothes and representing myself well in social situations (okay, I'm not quite as sterling in this latter regard, but do well enough); can roll with conversations of most all political and religious persuasions. Granted, I'm still more white collar than blue collar, more urban than rural, more coastal than interior, more left than right, more politically correct than not—but I mostly don't mind being around those who I'm different than and able to weather situations I'm unfamiliar with. And, perhaps most importantly, I often find those people and situations fascinating.

That, I've come to believe, is one of the secret weapons of dealing with an uncertain future: finding a certain fascination and interest in the elements of the world that are unfamiliar or unlike your own. The future we face is one of disruption, which means that much of it is going to feel unfamiliar. I am firmly convinced at this point that it's also going to feature a lot of social and cultural fissures, strange alliances and oppositions, social reorganization, and cultural shifts that those of us who have grown up with certain familiar social dichotomies over the last several decades are going to find surprising and in many ways disconcerting. Getting out ahead of these changes by opening oneself up to the different types of people and cultures out there is a good way to make at least partial peace with a coalescing future that is going to be very unlike what we have known up until now. The benefit of that, as well, is that it makes for a far more interesting and expansive world, which, in my experience, makes for much better living.

Here's the broader challenge of a generalist, though: any coherent life needs its limits. Part of the reason I enjoy being a generalist is because I want so much out of my life. What do I want? It's simple, really: I want to write and publish essays and novels, farm or homestead, spend copious amounts of time with my wife, read lots of books, eat good food, drink good drink, and be outside, all while making a comfortable living and feeling connected to the living earth. Easy. What's not so easy, of course, is figuring out how to compromise a life out of those many desires, especially in a world so bizarre as the one we find ourselves confronted with today.

It would be easier if I picked a couple of those desires and pursued them wholeheartedly, but I don't seem to work that way (and yes, a good chunk of this is about discipline more than it is about any inherent nature of myself). Which of them appeal to me most vacillate over time, and I have a hard time giving up any of them, believing there's some way to fit them all into my life. To some degree, I think there is—but it requires both some compromise and most certainly not being a specialist in all of them. There just isn't enough time (or personal attention span, for that matter) for me to master them all.

There are certain ones I continue to come back to more often than others, though. One is easy: my wife. Again and again, I find myself returning to the joy and comfort of my marriage to Kate, and if I'm going to specialize in anything, it's our relationship (and yes, I am definitely going to specialize in that). The other, though, is growing food, which has the added benefit of going a long way toward providing me time outside and connection to the living earth. I have done this through farming, of course, but also through gardening (though never to the degree that I think I will in the darkness of January and February). It is this desire that returned me to my friends' farm in the early days of May and will take me there many more times throughout the summer. The way that farming continues to this day to echo its way throughout my life, impacting perhaps every major element of who and I am and what my life holds, is one of the reasons I continue to return to it each year in some way or another, and also a good part of what makes it continue to feel to me as though it's a crucial element of my time here on earth. Growing food still is elemental to me as a person, even though I do much less of it now than I once did.

The trick here is in figuring out how to grow food while still making a living. In theory, one should be able to make the latter while doing the former—in a sane society, certainly that would be the case—but the context is crucial. There are many people in many places who simply can't make a living growing food, or for whom it would be theoretically possible but incredibly hard. I fall somewhat in that category; my current situation is not very amenable to making a living by growing and selling food. That doesn't mean it's impossible by any means, but I have yet to piece together a clear and coherent strategy on how to make it happen within the context of the rest of my life. Therefore, I seek out for the moment other ways to grow food, such as by gardening and helping my friends out with their farming, finding opportunities to steal moments into that magical world of coaxing food from soil.

Perhaps, I sometimes think, I can make a modest living writing and spend a good chunk of my non-writing time farming and homesteading. Or perhaps I can piece together a living by doing both, as a few lucky others have. I do not rule out the possibility, but I recognize that this hope is even more ambitious than simply making a living farming.

And so again I come back to the life I know today, of a professional day job that pays the bills with a handful of generalist side gigs that fill out my time and bring certain satisfactions I might not otherwise know. It works, in its way, but holds it's challenges, too, not least of all is the way I try too often to overbook myself. It's an ask of my wife, whose generosity is both impressive and key. And it's an ask of myself, too, who is sometimes battered by my desire to have a little bit of everything. This I sometimes think of as the curse of the generalist, but I think it's a curse that I'm willing to live with. At the end of the day, I'm sustained by the way I am able to dabble and piece together my life from a wide range of sometimes disparate pieces, and that variety of experience is key to keeping me engaged and invigorated.

‡‡

Ultimately, this is just one more challenge of our times. As the world changes around us and promises more dramatic changes to come, we have to balance which world to firmly plant our feet in—or, alternately, how to straddle a few different worlds. I consider myself as doing the latter, trying to keep my balance as the ground buckles beneath me, hoping that as its terrain becomes more clear, I can adjust accordingly to stay standing. To be honest, I don't know if this strategy will work or even if it's best. But I do know what makes me happy, and it's long been my belief that the intersection of utility and pleasure is a place to seek out. So I grow food, I write and read, I make money working a job I mostly enjoy, even if it doesn't bring me the same kind of joy and satisfaction as farming, and I most importantly make a life together with Kate. Aside from the latter, I don't know which of these lives will stay and which will fall by the wayside as both the world and I evolve. But somewhere in there, I think, is the structure of my future. In staying a generalist, perhaps I'll find that future easier to discover in the years ahead—and perhaps I'll find the journey there more rewarding, as well.

— *Portland, Oregon*
May 7, 2018

Into the Ruins is published quarterly by Figuration Press. We publish deindustrial science fiction that explores a future defined by natural limits, energy and resource depletion, industrial decline, climate change, and other consequences stemming from the reckless and shortsighted exploitation of our planet, as well as the ways that humans will adapt, survive, live, die, and thrive within this future.

One year, four issue subscriptions to *Into the Ruins* are $39. You can subscribe by visiting intotheruins.com/subscribe or by mailing a check made out to Figuration Press to:

Figuration Press / 3515 SE Clinton Street / Portland, OR 97202

To submit your work for publication, please visit intotheruins.com/submissions or email submissions@intotheruins.com.

All issues of *Into the Ruins* are printed on paper, first and foremost. Electronic versions will be made available as high quality PDF downloads. Please visit our website for more information. The opinions expressed by the authors do not necessarily reflect the opinions of Figuration Press or *Into the Ruins*. Except those expressed by Joel Caris, since this is a sole proprietorship. That said, all opinions are subject to (and commonly do) change, for despite the Editor's occasional actions suggesting the contrary, it turns out he does not know everything and the world often still surprises him.

EDITOR-IN-CHIEF
JOEL CARIS

DESIGNER
JOEL CARIS

WITH THANKS TO
JOHN MICHAEL GREER
SHANE WILSON
CHUCK MASTERSON
OUR SUBSCRIBERS

SPECIAL THANKS TO
KATE O'NEILL

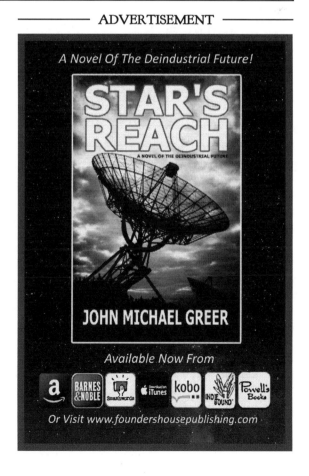

CONTRIBUTORS

A mathematician and bibliophile with a mystical streak, **HANNES ROLLIN** has turned to writing fiction as yet another means of approaching the convoluted conundrums of our time. When he's not immersed in the world of words, he eats, sleeps, and meditates somewhere in the northwestern province of Germany, with or without his wife and two kids.

RITA RIPPETOE is author of *Booze and the Private Eye: Alcohol in the Hard-Boiled Novel* and *A Reappraisal of Jane Duncan: Sexuality, Race and Colonialism in the My Friends Novels*, both published by McFarland & Co. Rita received a PhD in English from the University of Nevada, Reno; a M.A. in English from CSU, Sacramento; and a B.A. in Anthropology from UC, Davis. She is a member of Mystery Writers of America and Sisters in Crime. Although she has lived as far afield as Los Angeles, Hawaii, Colorado and Vancouver, BC, she currently lives in the suburbs of Sacramento, California with two box turtles and a desert tortoise.

ALISTAIR HERBERT writes from a little house on the edge of Todmorden in West Yorkshire, where he lives with his partner and two young children. He studied creative writing at the University of Manchester and now works part time for a local government organisation—an occupation which has largely kept him out of trouble for thirteen years. His work has previously appeared in Comma Press' *Parenthesis* anthology, as well as in *Into the Ruins: Summer 2017* (Issue #6) and *Into the Ruins: Winter 2018* (Issue #8).

W. JACK SAVAGE is a retired broadcaster and educator. He is the author of seven books, including *Imagination: The Art of W. Jack Savage* (wjacksavage.com). To date, more than fifty of Jack's short stories and over seven hundred of his paintings and drawings have been published worldwide. Jack and his wife Kathy live in Monrovia, California. Jack is, as usual, responsible for this issue's cover art.

JOEL CARIS is a gardener and homesteader, occasional farmer, passionate advocate for local and community food systems, sporadic writer, voracious reader, sometimes prone to distraction and too attendant to detail, a little bit crazy, a cynical optimist, and both deeply empathetic toward and frustrated with humanity. He is your friendly local editor and publisher. As a reader of this journal and perhaps other writings of his, he hopes you don't too easily tire of his voice and perspective. He lives in Oregon with his all-too-amazing wife.

DAVID ENGLAND is a ponderer, generalist, and student-of-everything who, in the words of his daughter, "does math for a living." Following a nomadic childhood typical among military families, and supplemented by wanderings of his own, he now resides in the well-rooted community of Two Rivers, Wisconsin (birthplace of the ice cream sundae) with his wife Anne, her incredible artwork, and the half-dozen or so unwritten novels which have taken up residence inside his head over the years.

At sixty-three years of age, **JEANNE LABONTE** is a lifelong resident of northern New Hampshire. Her day job is with a small mail order business (to pay the bills) but her main interests are writing, drawing, gardening, reading and publishing personal observations about them, as well as about the beauty of the local environment, in her blog New Hampshire Green Leaves, located at jeannemlabonte.com

DAMIAN MACRAE spent his formative years on a dairy farm watching Star Trek and reading dusty paperbacks from the likes of King, Vance and Herbert. Fleeing the family farm weeks after completing high school he has worked various IT jobs across Australia before moving to Hobart, Tasmania to study surveying where he learned to brew beer, stew rabbit and keep chooks. After two years working underground and a volunteer assignment in Laos he now resides in Christchurch, New Zealand with his partner. In between working and writing he dreams of owning a small farm, perhaps with some chooks. Occasionally, he threatens to build a wooden sail-boat.

LETTERS TO THE EDITOR

Dear Editor,

I very much enjoyed reading your introduction to *Into the Ruins: Winter 2018* ("The Problem With 'Change'"). I suspect that for many writers the business of explaining the story's world can feel at odds with the business of telling the story's *story*. It's no accident that in some of the most powerful stories we have—those of our various folk traditions—the world building is almost entirely absent; there is a castle, or a village, or a hut in a forest. That's often really all you get, and the rest of the story is, well, story. With the kinds of fictions which look to the future, though, a large part of the story's point is that its world is new to the reader, so the author must invest precious words in bringing that altered world to life, often before the story even really begins. The author must dance constantly between progressing the plot and describing the world or introducing ideas.

The balancing act is difficult to control—which I suppose is part of the beauty when you see it working well—and I think the short story's form doesn't necessarily help. Where in a novel the author can take a few pages here and there to draw out details of the world without their necessarily having immediate impact on the plot or characters, the short story is always pushing you to focus on one thing, one moment and its immediate surroundings, which makes it difficult to tell the story well and also paint the world fully enough to demonstrate the kind of complexity a world ought to have. Without bringing the setting to life, you're not envisaging future worlds; without bringing the human story to life, you're not writing compelling fiction. It begins to feel much easier to just say "The nukes went off and now mutants roam the wastes!" and set your story in a culturally familiar setting. But there are other ways, as we have seen.

The easy way out of this trap is of course to write novels (preferably "literary fiction," in whose vast playground pretty much anything goes; my own favourite example might be the mutant hamsters in David Foster Wallace's *Infinite Jest*), but another possibility I've been pursuing—taking my lead instead from M. John Harrison's *Viriconium* stories and Haruki Murakami's *After the Quake*—is to tell the same world repeatedly in different stories, from different angles. In the first drafts of my story "The Change Year" (*Into the Ruins: Winter 2018*), I tried to cram everything about my new world into one story, and I had to give up; the piece was becoming a catalogue more than a story. To fix it I stripped it down to only those details of the world which served the plot, and then went in search of other stories to show the rest of that world. The bureaucrat in the city and the churchwoman on the coast have only the vaguest awareness of each other's worlds, and neither knows what life looks like in the abandoned towns nearby, but writing three separate pieces allows the reader to see the contrasts and eventually piece together the whole world. Like a painted or photographed triptych, the pieces are separate, their stories are whole, but they inform each other for the reader about the particular ways in which a place and its surroundings interact, and the particular ways its people can choose to be people. This, at least, is the intention.

Because—if you'll forgive the shift from questions of craft to questions of content—I'm coming to think that it's not as simple as merely avoiding the extremes of "instantaneous collapse" and "technological breakthrough"; to make matters worse, I have a third trope to add to your list: "the same, but worse." For an example, I might pick my own story "The Rig and the Wave" (*Into the Ruins: Summer 2017*), which arguably leans on "the same, but worse" just as much as some of your essay's targets lean on "instantaneous collapse"; my characters still think in the same ways we think today, and somehow manage to adapt to a different world without their ruling morality or philosophy undergoing much change. Only my unseen villain seems significantly altered by the changed world. I think this is just as serious a problem for forward-looking fiction as that of the collapse/progress tropes; I would argue—and I draw support from several of your contributors' stories in previous issues—that the people in our dramatically different worlds can't continue to think and behave the same way we do in our own world. Morality, culture, and philosophy are shaped by the ways in which world, community and individual humans interact, and we should expect our people—not just the villains but the protagonists, families, leaders, everyone—to be as different from ourselves as their worlds are from ours.

I would go so far as to say that this re-imagining of what it can mean to be human is, for me, the major project of speculative fiction in our age. The question becomes not only "How does the world change?", but also "How does the world change *us*?"

With thanks and best wishes,

Alistair Herbert
Todmorden, United Kingdom

Dear Editor,

It is fun to fantasize about a future community, let's say two centuries from now, where everyone lives peacefully in isolated farm communities and rides horses. A writer can create a pretty good plot out of that, and I'm as guilty as anyone. But stop, Joel has a point. In the real world civilizations don't change that quickly or easily.

Sources of energy don't disappear overnight. Incrementally, they become harder to obtain and more expensive. Substitutes are found and natural sources such as water and wind turbines, and tidal surges are tapped. As costs increase, energy use is reduced. Manufacturing doesn't stop, but it does become increasingly costly. Locating near to a natural energy source becomes desirable. Labor intensive operations, small workshops, and home-made goods become more common.

But we still have computers, planes, ships and locomotives. We haven't forgotten how to do things, we still have libraries and digital information storage. But everything is increasingly more difficult and expensive than it used to be. In principle we could build a moon rocket, but we don't because the cost in energy and materials would be too great.

Thing is, if we (in the future farm community) resign ourselves to living with candlelight and horses we will be overrun by those who don't. In the changing world energy creates power. Those who have access to the dwindling energy pool must be armed and vigilant. For safety our rural community has to be allied with a larger political organization, one that is always at war or about to war to either obtain energy or protect our own.

Al Sevcik
Tampa, Florida

Dear Editor,

Walking the talk. That is what I aspire and lead my acquaintances to do. If you were looking over my shoulder you'd see us building soil for growing food. You'd watch and help us build solar dryers, and use freeze-drying to preserve food. Maybe you would assist in building and using a "closet type" root cellar in our conventional cellar and showing others how to do that. Our group is supporting others in enterprises of hydroponics, methane production from food scraps, and implementation of that gas in cooking and heating. We are in action filling the root cellar closet with products we produce from crops we grow, including fermented products like kimchi, sauerkraut, staples like potatoes, and beets. We give away the excess food on a monthly schedule. We are showing others how to make fruit ciders and fermented products like hard cider and vinegar. We've been growing and grinding corn and figuring out how to make it nutritious by releasing niacin. We are passing along the technologies that my parents, grandparents, and other people have used to grow food, preserve food, and raise chickens, sheep, goats, pigs, to collect fibers like wool and flax, and how to spin and weave and process fiber. In each step of the way we are engaging others in this process, mostly young people and even kids. In turn these youngsters have passed on technology, too. We are active in showing youngsters and anyone interested in paper making, tanning hides, building tiny houses, and educating kids in timber framing, cordwood house building, and other technologies like saw sharpening. Our little spark of activity in our area has also been actively pursuing advocacy for food sovereignty, land preservation, and respect for and support of indigenous native populations as well as permaculture projects.

Some of us reject using fossil fuel to accomplish many tasks, and others of us utilize the fuels for accomplishing heavy tasks like post hole-digging, firewood-harvesting for heating and cooking, and making berms and swales. Terraforming to stop soil loss that will last millennia is a good use of fossil fuel.

The important factor in all of these endeavors is to be in action doing them in our local community. We have been made aware of the need to accomplish this through our association with and practices that are outlined by the Transition Movement, which was our entry into all of these endeavors. One of our goals is to cre-

ate a community that is resilient in the face of the black swans that may have threatening sway. And guess what? It is FUN!

Thanks for helping to create stories about what the world may look like in the future. Your latest issues in 2017 and 2018, as well as the works of John Michael Greer and others, are prime examples. It's really important for people to envision what their little neighborhood may look like in a thousand years and to pass this vision along to generations, and the importance of inventing ways of being to perhaps help us to live lives that nurture the relatedness of all beings on earth.

Larry Ulfik
Saugerties, New York
applewoodscientific.com

Dear Editor,

I really liked your introduction ("The Problem With 'Collapse,'" *Into the Ruins: Winter 2018*) and raising the question about collapse versus slide. I think we will eventually get to a place in the literature where we can just jump into the lower industrial level without having to mention what happened. I do wonder though—each civilization as it is dying probably *does* think of itself as the end of the world, or at least as the biggest civilization ever to fall. Humans are just like that. It's one reason I appreciate your continuing this magazine, because it allows people to have a *different* perspective, to actually consider that indeed we are just one of many civilizations that have risen and fallen. I think that is a big reason that I mostly set my stories pretty far into the future, after people have in fact come to grips with a different level of industrialization —it's more interesting to me how people normalize the new way of life then how they handle any kind of downslide. Perhaps I'm just not skilled enough to picture that subtle decline so that it's there and yet not the main story.

Cathy McGuire
Sweet Home, Oregon

Dear Editor,

Hi.

Your piece on collapse ("The Problem With 'Collapse,'" *Into the Ruins: Winter 2018*) was interesting—however, irrelevant.

Collapse is purely perceptual.

Imagine the difference in verticality from one dash to another is the difference from our present high tech situation and the "lower" dash is hunter/gatherer/horticulturalism (i.e. how humans lived for several hundred thousand years).

So, there is this: Each space equals one day.

- - - - - - -

- - - - - - -

So, in twenty-four hours we go from watching Netflix to chasing buffalo. Result? Extinction. Billions die in weeks.

Now, each dash equals one year.

- - - - - - -

- - - - - - - -

So, a year or two goes by between coconut ice cream and spearing fish. Result? Near extinction, billions die off.

Now each dash equals ten years.

- - - - - -

- - - - - - -

Billions still die off, but it's not nearly as insane; over a period of ten years people set up systems that are renewable and continuous.

Add a zero.

In one hundred years, and this is very important: NO ONE WILL REMEMBER.

Generational amnesia sets in. So if you go from Bugatti Veryon to horseback in one hundred years, the signifiers of the past (especially architecture) will be present, but the exigencies of life will render them mythic and divorced from experience. Now make it two hundred years.

No one will be alive to remember what it was like—therefore *the collapse never happened.*

Events only occur insofar as there is an observer and a consideration of contrast. No contrast: no event. No reportage: no discussion. It's kind of like death. You won't know death. You will experience dying, but death itself is external to your possible experiences —any experience you have is, by definition, a part of your life. Therefore, you will never experience death. You will only experience life.

Same with society—if the reduction in complexity is drawn out long enough, it won't experience collapse. It will experience hard times, times that occupy a series of generations, however, it won't understand "collapse."

A friend of mine is from Cuba and she said that when they experienced an energy collapse with the failure of the Soviet Union, things were tough. Everyone was very upset and the hardship was immense. But after about six months, you learn to smile again.

Collapse is perceptual. Once you internalise that, you can be more gentle with the horror. Your rage will dissipate.

That doesn't mean that industrial civilisation isn't destined to disappear. It certainly is. But the transition from Netflix to spear fishing can take a long time, and if it is long enough—no one will notice.

This means that we could easily have massive energy crises with billions living in wreckage *and* totally weird Artificial Intelligence devices. Desperate starvations from ecological disasters *and* self driving vehicles.

As much as I love *Into the Ruins*, there is a certain romanticism of the dire within your rationale, and it shows in your sense of collapse. I would suggest that in five hundred years we will very likely be chasing buffalo for a living, *and* there will

have been no "collapse." Billions will die off. Corporations will disappear. Cities will be emptied. But no collapse will occur, as none was noticed. It was just "bad times"—and then you learn to smile again, followed by more bad times, and then you learn to smile again—wash, rinse, repeat.

Henry Warwick
Toronto, Ontario
kether.com

Dear Henry,

Thanks for your response to my Editor's Introduction. However—and perhaps I did not get this point across well enough in my essay—I agree with you, assuming I'm understanding you right. One of the things I'm criticizing is exactly what you're talking about: stories set in far future times that talk about "The Collapse" or some variant on that, as though it would be something these future people think about. It likely wouldn't. It would just be their world, and they wouldn't be judging it against our time day in and day out any more than we judge our current reality against cultures and societies from hundreds or thousands of years ago. (Yes, those comparisons are made on occasion, but they are mostly ignored by the culture at large and certainly do not serve as a broad-based and common cultural preoccupation.)

That's why I titled the essay what I did. I want more stories doing exactly what you're talking about— showing us future cultures and societies and characters living in vastly different worlds than ours who aren't comparing their world to ours because they probably don't even know about our world, outside whatever myths about us have built up over the decades, centuries, and so on. It can be challenging, of course, because authors know that the readers of these stories *will* be comparing the future society they envision to our own—but their characters generally shouldn't be. One of the potential benefits of writing a story for *Into the Ruins* should be a certain expectation that the readers will understand the point of the project enough that less hand-holding is necessary, and that if a story depicts a future society radically different than ours and also not conforming to the more common assumptions about what the future will be like (space travel! galactic colonization!), the author is under no obligation to explain the physical constraints that carved out that culture in the however-many-years from now to then because it should be *assumed* that our culture's usual expectations for the future are nonsense.

Sincerely,

Joel Caris, Editor
Portland, Oregon

Dear Editor,

My fiancé and I are getting married this summer, and plan to have a table filled with wedding photos of our parents and grandparents. On the wall of my family home are wedding portraits from great- and even great-great grandparents, but, other than their names and their fantastic outfits, I know next to nothing about them. The two of us pondered: in a hundred years, if our wedding photo has the good fortune to be passed down to our great-great descendants, will they know anything about us? Mostly likely not. Other than perhaps a fascination with their ancestral lineage, they probably won't care about us at all. No, they'll have parents, and perhaps kids, much more precious to them than two odd looking "millenials" from the turn of the previous century, deep in their family tree. This reflection begs the question: why should we care about them, or the future they will inherit? Unless you're part of a royal lineage or destined for fame or infamy, you'll be lucky if a future member of your own family knows anything about you. At worst, perhaps my Facebook page will live on as an eternal epitaph to the wasteful energy use of the early twenty-first century.

So if the world forgets me, as it will most all of us, why not just enjoy "business as usual" and let Ross the IV pick up the pieces? This narrative is an easy out, but false. It is part and parcel of the belief that humanity is somehow apart from nature, able to control it on the way up, now helpless to change it on the way down. By planting a tree, can't I provide shade for the grandson of my grandson? By keeping a library, can I not provide knowledge for those after me willing to learn? Even through my own death, can I not spark an awakening in my childrens' minds to the reality of their own mortality, inspiring a quest for truth, just as my father's passing did for me (without which I would probably not be writing this letter today)? Just as the long collapse is an incremental one, so is our ability on a human time scale to effect change, for good or bad. I won't save the world in one fell swoop, but damn if I can't leave this mortal coil without casting a positive ripple for good into the far future.

Ross Bridgeman
Whitefish, Montana
rossbridgeman.com

Dear Editor,

I find that the biggest and most important aspect of collapse is that it doesn't happen over the weekend. I have spent (wasted) a lot of energy worrying about aspects of collapse over which I do not have direct control. (For example, decisions made by world leaders that draw us ever closer to unpleasant changes.)

I believe there is hopefulness, or at least faith, in the inevitability of life, death, rebirth and studying both history and evolution certainly provides a basis for that. Certainly disasters like hurricanes, bombing, floods happen quickly, measured often in minutes and hours, and they take a huge toll on those in their direct path. Survivors survive, persist, and rebuild. Their day to day lives after disaster include many of the same dramas and joys as those of us who have not had to endure the challenges they face.

I find it easier to stay in the present. Start each day with gratitude for the relatively clean air I breathe (here in NYC), the hot and cold water that runs from my taps, the abundance of food in my kitchen, a warm house, people I love, and work I enjoy.

I have begun preparing for an uncertain future with what I fondly refer to as the "apocalypse bag" that doubles as a camping bag. I can start a fire with trash and a match, and I always have a few boxes of those. I can cook. I recognize common edible plants in my area. And best of all I can spin, weave, and knit so I could trade clothing for all manner of other goods. I can also brew some basic mildly alcoholic beverages and expect that might be good for trading as well. In the meantime I enjoy practicing these Stone Age technologies for the marvels that they are, and the potential future they have.

I've spent the last two years working on a book called *Sustainable Health: Simple Habits to Transform Your Life*. The publisher (W. W. Norton) plans to have it out by end of September. I mention you, *Into the Ruins*, and John Michael Greer, at various points throughout and thank-you heartily for your ideas that helped me on this journey. The book aims to help all of us take our health back into our own hands by changing simple habits of playing, sleeping, eating, working, and loving.

Keep up the good work.

Susan L. Roberts, MDiv, OTR/L
Flushing, New York
susanlroberts.com

Dear Editor,

It seems a response is in order to G.Kay Bishop's most recent letter directed for me. To wit:

Yo, G.Kay—

Sōðlíce iċ ne wēnde þætte iċ wordsweordum wið swylċre cræftiġre bōcestran lāce! Iċ hycge þēah þatte þū medemiest tō nāganne þæt mæne folc swylċum abroðenum Angliscē swā swā man in þām strǣtum þissum dagum spricþ. Sorhlīċ ġewlǣtedness is hit, þǣr sēo wuldorlice rīfnis endunga namworda is swā āwerode tō nāwihte būtan þām seldan s. Ic nāt hū æġðre lēodas understandaþ ōðre.[1]

But on the other hand . . . when I think about picking up that torch of old grammar from the centuries of writers of the past, with all its lucidity and complexity and self-contradiction, so I can carry it forward, still burning, into a bright future—well, it just seems awful boring. Why should they have gotten to have all the fun? In the 1600s people were abandoning yᵉ old *eateth & drinketh* forms pell-mell, spurning the venerable *thou*, and making an untrackable hash of their vowels—and the while, replacing each old convolution with some exciting new one: new words by the literal thousands, a bizarre singular-plural

---

[1] *Truly I didn't reckon that I play at word-swords with such a formidable scholar! I do wonder, however, that you deign to address the people in such degenerate English as is spoken in the streets these days. A sorry bastardization it is, where the glorious old profusion of noun endings has worn away to nothing but an occasional s. I don't know how people understand each other.*

you, and so forth. Why does Shakespeare get to thumb his nose at his yesteryear's grammarians while making up words and saying things like "Uncle me no uncles," and get called *inventive* and *superior word dude*, but when we try and pull those kind of shenanigans there's always someone waiting to tell us we missed the deadline for fun?

I for one am not really feeling sticking to the past's particular profusion of confusion when us modern weirdos are more than capable of conjuring our own. Sure, English doesn't have an ablative anymore, but we've got plenty neat toys the ablatizers didn't. We can combine modals in more ways than we used to could, and it looks like some intriguing new ones finna come out the hood into other people's English. Plus verbing. *Do you even grammar?* In analyzing some of the Salishan languages of the Pacific Northwest, linguists have been at a loss as to how to distinguish nouns, adjectives, and verbs, because any given word that seems to be in one of those categories can be used as the other two, too. Could English be on the way to a future that fascinating? If it is, I'm sure not tryna stand in its way.

All of which is to say, if you're putting out a battle cry for the war over changing language, you've sent your communiqué to the wrong side's officer. (But my army has the advantage anyway: most of your soldiers have already been dead for years.)

There may be one place, though, where you and me can yet find common ground. I still like the old *literally*. Not because it's immoral for a word's meaning to change, mind you, but because, in this specific case, I have yet to discover another way to point out an accidental pun or Freudian slip with anything close to the laconic bang you get when you say, ". . . Literally." I'll pluralize as modernly as I dern well please, and encourage others to shake off their corroded old Roman shackles too, but that one will probably always raise my hackles. Wherever those are. I hope that, at least, lets you rest easier about our future imperfect.

Chuck Masterson
Minneapolis, Minnesota

Into the Ruins welcomes letters from our readers. We encourage thoughtful commentary on the contents of this issue, the themes of the magazine, and humanity's collective future. Readers may email their letters to editor@intotheruins.com or mail them to:

Figuration Press
3515 SE Clinton Street
Portland, OR 97202

Please include your full name, city and state, and an email or phone number. Only your name and location will be printed with any accepted letter.

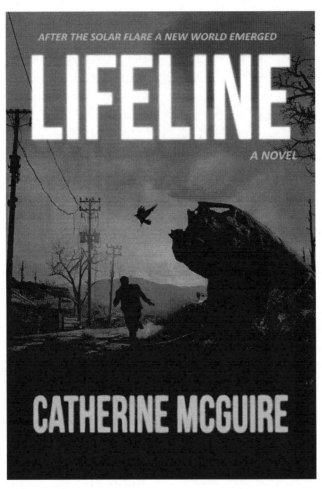

Into the Ruins: Year One
Issues #1–4

Available now for just $43
Shipped free anywhere in the United States

Visit intotheruins.com/year-one
or send a check for $43
made out to Figuration Press to:

Figuration Press
3515 SE Clinton Street
Portland, OR 97202

Into the Ruins: Year Two
Issues #5-8

Available now for just $43
Shipped free anywhere in the United States

Visit intotheruins.com/year-two
or send a check for $43
made out to Figuration Press to:

Figuration Press
3515 SE Clinton Street
Portland, OR 97202

If ordering by mail, don't forget to include the name and address of where you want your package sent. Please include an email address or phone number for notification of order fulfillment and shipment.

STORIES

ARCHIVE

BY ALISTAIR HERBERT

HOW DOES MEMORY WORK?

Deer forced their way into the gardens and laid waste—early spring, every creature hungry, and understandable what they did but unforgivable they'd been able to do it. Those fields which lay inland from the church were left hopeless: roots without leaves, all winter green gone, thin deer still taking chances and hunting for scraps. As a result the work had been abundant. There was more meat to cut and cure than they would have wanted, less food to come in summer, and every bed in the gardens to work over again in attempted salvage. Holly enjoyed the garden work— and, though she pretended otherwise, enjoyed that something exciting was happening and someone else was to blame—but it took time, and required that she use her small spaces of reflection not to further build her knowledge but just to maintain it. That, perhaps, was no bad thing; the familiar run of breathing, exercise, meditation and prayer helped to centre her again.

As one of the church's faith keepers, her role was to accurately preserve religious exercises and pass them on, and her personal practice differed from the historical text in only one respect: every time she inhaled to commence an exercise, she thought of her mother. The memory swam up each time from nowhere, but it had happened from the start: the first time she practised after her mother's departure, nine years old and newly initiated, alone in the world for the first time and desperately homesick, she saw her mother's shape performing the actions ahead of her. The entirety of the exercise appeared as she took her first breath, all at once, and then the shape vanished. She had been ashamed, and only revealed it too late to her mentor. The mentor told her that the damage was done; she should accept that her mother's shape had, for her, become part of the exercise, only remembering in her preservation work that it existed only for her, and was not an essential component.

Because this was how the exercises worked: repetition, the slow establishment of useful pathways for the self to travel, and her pathway was now half built, her mother a part of it.

The exercise was her whole reason for coming here—the thing her mother had wanted her to learn—but with time she had become more a part of the faith than her mother had even known existed of the faith; the cherished "two selves in one home" had become one tiny part of the larger thing she now served. She knew it well because she was a faith keeper and practised daily, but others might not practice it at all. The church was a vast thing, and, while roles were less distinct than she had first believed, they remained meaningful: no world keeper could hope to know everything Holly kept in herself—though she would advise them as often as they asked—just as no faith keeper would ever be so expert in the work of the land. The business of actually knowing something was the business of practising it endlessly, treading it into yourself until you couldn't not know it, and that was only possible for any one person to do with a very few things. The more knowledge you took on, the less you knew it.

This was what attracted her to the place even years later. Her mother had been dismayed that she wanted to stay, that she would limit her life so early and tie it to this place, but when she arrived she had felt a new self kindle inside her, and had known her wish. She was too young to know better but she didn't regret it. Her world came alive in the church: the motley gated freehold, the shifting dunes, the waiting murmur of the sea. It felt more real somehow than the patchwork city. There was more work, less comfort, but the ground was less flat and more alive.

After practice she ate and took visits, or worked lessons with guests. If the farm needed no help she got time to herself. She wasn't ambitious: she wanted to serve her role and be good at it, and she loved the church, but she didn't require praise and so she disdained the debates with which some of her colleagues filled their spare days. She preserved the exercises. Others tended the archives, worked the earth, or governed the place, and they lived together, maybe three hundred people not counting guests and scholars.

She felt drowsy between bursts of energy, struggling to adapt to the temporarily meat-heavy diet, and when an afternoon finally arrived with no tasks to fill it she found herself bored, unable to study, and somehow came to be loitering idly near the stair to the archives. She felt cat-like, relaxed and alert, slightly indignant about moving around but enjoying it all the same. She was surprised to find herself spending her first free afternoon roaming the church's dim corridors, hemmed in by walls when she could be outside, and hoping to see someone she had decided she disliked. The newcomer's throwaway remarks had done their work: she was interested despite herself, and beneath the tranquility of her movement along the halls lurked eagerness suppressed only by good practice. Being suppressed so, she would have been able to inspect it, but she didn't: she knew what she would find, and she had dismissed it repeatedly already because she didn't care for it. It warned that the newcomer would bring her trouble.

Yet here she was.

He was a man, which was unusual in itself. Even without that distinction he would have stood out: he was obviously a commoner, the kind of person her parents would have steered her around in the city—and his type never showed up here. She was both curious and repulsed: it wasn't that he looked poor, but that he was city poor, town poor, and had somehow escaped his proper place. The idea that anyone like that could get out of the slums and swagger past her at dinner on the north coast was difficult to understand. She was surprised and a little ashamed to find that this was what she thought, but it was true.

He had caught her watching him one morning in the gardens and of course he then walked over to greet her. She was resting on the benches and he sat down opposite, neither asking permission nor attempting an introduction.

"You just sit around all day, do you?" Again she saw how out of place he was. Nobody spoke like that. She saw no reason to reply—it was her rest day, and she was resting—but eventually she had to look at him again and when she did so she found him looking back with half a smile. He was probably about her own age, tall with narrow shoulders and stick legs, but thicker arms and an expansive posture. He had dark hair which he'd clearly washed but not thought to brush, and wore borrowed church clothes which looked wrong on him. "Go on," he said. "Say hello."

"I ought to ask," she answered, "how of all good churchwomen I led you to choose me to impose yourself upon, and how I might avoid repeating the mistake." He laughed—no cunning smile or small chuckle, but a plain laugh.

"Easy. Of all the women—and indeed men—I've looked at in this place, you're the only one who looked back without trying to pretend you weren't looking. That means we'll get along. That's fire in your belly."

She lowered her eyes reflexively, instinct telling her she was in the wrong. She had already been impossibly rude. But she had more than one instinct, and when he spoke again she met his eyes and let herself be drawn into his talk.

"So," he began again.

"So," she answered, mollified. She knew how to be polite. "Hello." And he smiled.

"Ask me," he said. She gave him a puzzled look. "Oh, come on. You know. Ask me the question. Who am I, what do I think I'm doing, how on earth did someone like me end up sitting in your holy garden. It's okay, you can ask. I'll tell you."

"I suppose if I wasn't here," Holly answered, "you'd tell the trees." She leaned back a little, and he leaned in.

"All right. You convinced me. I'll tell you my secrets. It started back in the patchwork city . . ."

He was supposedly a research student, gathering material from the archives on instruction from his mentor, but in fact he had other intentions, and was hoping to solve some forbidden historical question and win his own fame. She couldn't quite guess if he was disobeying the mentor, or if the mentor himself was a fabrication.

"This seems like a dangerous conversation for you," she said when he paused. "You're risking your career and your secret on the chance to trade stories with someone you don't even know?"

He grinned. "It's not a risk. I know you're not going to tell anyone. In fact, I think you're going to help me." She began to feel, belatedly, that she was losing control of her situation. Exercises came to mind, breathing patterns, meditations, movements, ready to begin their familiar practice and help her realign. But she pressed on, too far gone now to step back.

"Why?"

"Because of that fire in your belly, that thing which makes you hold my gaze when I walk past, when nobody else does. Because I can see it in there, hiding: a part of you which doesn't quite fit this world." He stood carefully, extricating himself from the bench. "Tell me," he said, "how much do you actually know about the founders?"

"The founders?" She was surprised. "Everyone knows—"

He cut her off. "Exactly. Which means, once you've thought about it, if I'm right about you, you'll want to find out a few things. You'll wonder what secret I know." He turned to leave and then, turning back, flashed her one last smile. "I'll see you around, I'm sure. Thanks for the snack." She looked down at the bench and saw that he had stolen her apple.

"Getting curious?"

She jumped.

She had always found the expression strange when she came across it in the texts. It wasn't unusual for archaic idioms to see opposite in wording to their meaning— to "make a saving" usually meant to spend some money, to "reach out" meant to stay put and send messages, to "do everything in your power" meant to do very little, and so on—but this one was harder to trace to its provenance. In Holly and everyone she knew, the instant reaction to a sudden shock was stillness and a stabilising breath. That didn't happen this time, though: she flinched from the sound, and her body prepared to fight. When she turned to face him her hands were clenched into fists. The old idiom wasn't flawed at all, then, she learned: it had simply had no place in her world. Whether it was him, her thoughts, or her diet which had created this new reaction for her, she didn't know. She found the feeling strange. Imagine living in a world where this experience was common enough to require its own idiom. She gathered herself.

"Sorry," he said, pleased with his effect on her. "But"—he paused more for effect than because of any genuine doubt—"I could use some help finding my way around, if you've nothing better to do. From someone sympathetic to my project."

He had her at a disadvantage again and she disliked the feeling, but her curiosity won out. "You're looking for something in the archives."

"That's right." He nodded.

"Something you think has been hidden."

He nodded.

"What?" she asked.

He smiled. "Why don't you show me which way to the founder's archive, and we'll find out together?"

They went down together and she thought she understood. He wanted her in the archives because nobody would surprise them there. The church's original basement had been partitioned into cells, then extended by cuts through bedrock and clay into a series of caverns, all lined with shelves. There were quiet spots and areas where all noise travelled, but in every corner you could hear the crash and hiss of the cellar door. It was waterproofed and as strong as the rock walls, and nobody could open or close it unheard.

She led him to the founder's archive: the cell in which original documents from the first years of the new world were preserved. It wasn't a heavily trafficked space, comprising items of historical value which had been exhausted of scholarly interest. Contemporary scholarship, as a rule, took more interest in periods whose history was less settled: recent history on the one hand and the puzzles of the oldest fragmentary texts on the other. Holly knew they wouldn't be interrupted, but she also doubted they could find anything so exciting in such well-known material.

What she was missing, he told her, was that this material had been considered well-known and settled from the moment it was born. Go back through the scholars' archives, he promised, and you'll find that the references to prior work never actually go away: the earliest surviving appraisal of the founder's archive discusses it as if all the work of interrogating it had already been done. Go further back, beyond that first assertion, and you find twenty years of silence. A generous mind, he said, would assume all of that missing work was simply not properly archived due to the more pressing troubles of the first years. But he thought that the work was never actually done; the first government had protected the churches in a time when other old institutions were falling, but nobody in the first government had wanted their own material studied, and the churches had been happy to comply with that wish. "What do you know about the founders?" he had asked her the first time they met, and laughed when she began to recount the story all people knew. He had a different version of the story.

The popular narrative told of a low level servant in the old world government who joined the people's revolution to help establish a stable new order. As the only defector, she was the only survivor, and her experience was invaluable. In deference to her stabilising role, the revolutionaries elected her first king, and she sadly died soon after. Her story was central to many tellings of the nation's birth: surrounded by thugs and inexperienced leaders, King Joan was one of few tangible personalities whose character had endured through history.

"What if," he asked her now in a soft voice, poring over the shelves and hunting for something, "what if that was all just a story, and the evidence of it was right under our noses?" But when he pulled down the text he was looking for she almost laughed. They hadn't needed to visit the archives for this: he was holding the founder's diary, probably the most copied text in the history of the new world.

"You wasted a journey coming all the way to the sea to read that," she started to tell him, but he ignored her and set the text down on the cell's small central reading plinth, drawing back the cover to attack the binding.

All archival texts were well bound, because binding properly in the first place was much cheaper than remaking damaged books, but the founder's notes were twice-bound because their original covering was half lost. The diary was what they technically classified a "substantial fragment": comprising two volumes, the first was missing its front pages and, with the pages unnumbered, the number of missing pages was unknown.

She realised belatedly what the newcomer was doing and moved to stop him, but he pushed her back easily. She coloured and moved around the plinth to face him. Then she saw that the diary itself was in no danger: he wasn't here to destroy it. He wasn't even here to read it. Scraps and splinters tumbled from the plinth as he shook the first section free of its cover and laid it out on one side of the plinth, the first page facing the light. His arm went to his coat, and from his clothing he drew a packet of old pages. He placed the stack down on the other side of the plinth and looked at it. The page on the right was the first of the founder's diary; the page on the left bore no words. Then he slipped his hands under the new papers and the diary, and pivoted the two together with a snap. They were one book.

This time Holly went still, and took a stabilising breath.

"Where did you get that?" she breathed. He didn't seem to hear her. He was caught in his own thought.

"Do you want to know," he asked her quietly, "the real story of King Joan?"

The air in the cell was so still she could feel her own body heat settling around her in the cold. She imagined the whole of the world must be paused above her as they stood there: world keepers' arms lifting branches to the fence; scribes with pens poised unfalling over half-written words; rivers stopped in motion, fleeing deer hanging in the air, frozen above the ground, brains frozen too, blades of grass stopped; nettles in the corners of fields reaching and never touching the approaching ankles, the ankles themselves not moving; the trouble in the south halted, lines of men and women interwoven, looking into each other's faces and unable to shout their orders. She tried to place herself among them, and as she played with it the feeling fell away. People were moving somewhere. Deer were moving. Nothing had paused, only herself and this man, this newcomer, and the book and the air in their cell.

"You're part of the resistance," she said, realising the significant of what he held. "You're one of their leaders."

"Say it louder," he deadpanned. "They didn't hear you in the guardhouse."

He met her gaze. He was relaxed, a little amused by the game, and flushed with the enjoyment of successfully engaging her, but there was something else there too. Defiance. A refusal to be taken for a joke. She sat up properly.

"You mean it. You want the war to get worse." She knew about the unrest near the city, though only a little. They said it was dissident factions taking advantage of hardship to rally support. She didn't see how fighting could make things better.

"I don't want the war at all," he answered. "But I'll fight it."

Then, in the stillness before either could speak again, she heard a strange slight sucking of air in the hallway and the deafening crash of the cellar door. Panicked herself, she watched him respond with swift, unhurried motions, bringing the newly made book into his jacket and collecting the scraps of binding, replacing the cover on the shelf so that the book would still seem to be there until someone looked for it. He led her out of the cell so they would be in the main hall when anyone saw them—and thereby no way to guess, she realised, which area they had been studying. In conversational tone he began telling her which texts he hoped to find next and where his mentor had told him he might find them, and as they passed the person who had entered—a junior record keeper whom Holly knew only vaguely—they exchanged nodded greetings and walked on. They sat at their pretended destination and read for some time before he suggested they break for the evening meal. She tried to relax.

At her door he followed her inside, held the door closed with his body, and murmured the story as briefly as he could manage it. King Joan was never a government official; she was a bandit, a warlord and petty thief, who ran riot across the country in the old world, sacking the old city twice but failing to hold it. She should have been a footnote; by the time the founder's diary officially commenced she was fifty years old, but she swooped in again during the riots and the civil war she hadn't caused, claiming the city before either side knew what was happening. From there she dealt with the rebels to write their history. The lost half of the diary—now proved authentic—confirmed it. The change laws which split their society by generation and gender, the constitution which fixed the behaviour of the new state: all of it was only a calculated move to ensure that her deputy was the only viable successor—a way to block rivals in the new state's first days and maintain a stranglehold on what wealth remained. It was accomplished under pretence of legitimacy, a belief that the woman at the heart of it was unifying a divided nation. It was untrue, he said, so the state was illegitimate. The book was a weapon of change.

Holly struggled to keep up. "The change law was what brought me here," she said at last. He looked at her, bewildered.

"The change law?" She could hear the surprise in his voice. "What does the change law have to do with anything?"

"That's what you're trying to end."

She saw in his eyes that she had misunderstood. But how was she to know? She had never seen any of the places he knew. For all she knew, he had never actually seen the city.

"Holly, the change law is city glamour—it barely touches us. It only matters now because it's a lie. I'm talking about the real power. The real change."

People are dying, he told her before he left the room. Actual people.

Think about it, he told her. I won't stay long now I've got what I came for. But, if you want, I can try and help you understand.

She struggled to keep up.

And then he said: your mother would have told you to listen.

A week later he returned to her room and said it was time. He thrust a packet into her hands and she took it, unthinking, wide eyed in the night. They had seen each other three times in that week, conversing as new acquaintances in the gardens. She knew his name—Lake—and more about his character than she had thought was there. She had failed to get from him what he knew about her mother. She had gently tried to warn him off from his plan, and he had tried to warm her up to his way of thinking. Now there was a reckoning before either had succeeded: the record keepers knew the book was missing, and they were searching the visitors' rooms. It wouldn't take long: every room was plain. Lake was asking her to take the book, King Joan's lost diary—and a stolen archival text – and the search was on. She wasn't sure which half of the book, if found in her hands, represented the worse crime.

"I don't trust you yet," he told her hurriedly, "but trusting you is the only way to do it. Once they've searched my room and I'm in the clear, I'll leave on the river path while it's still dark. You know they search guests, but they'll let me out for a walk if they're happy I've not taken anything. I'll wait at the first river junction. If you don't see me, just wait; I'll see you." He paused, breathless, and looked her over. "If you don't come, I'll assume you handed it over and told them what I told you.

That would be the best thing to do, after coming with me. But that way you'll never be the other you again."

He was gone.

She sat on the bed.

How does memory work? As an adult she could recover her childhood only in fragments. They called her birthplace the patchwork city, and she found herself remembering it in patchwork: the images were distinct; they belonged with each other but refused to interact.

There were shining towers in the centre, sprouting green on their south sides and dead on the north, looming over her as she rode the bus to a school she had entirely forgotten. Her head pressed against the glass of the bus window as she craned to see the tops of the buildings outlined against the sky, and never succeeded.

There was the back room of her parents' apartment, dimly carpeted and shimmering with the light of candles around decorated branches—holly. The feeling of the carpet on her bare feet as she ran to look again at the tree, her father muttering behind her, the tree serving as a focal point for an excitement which found no outlet.

There was her father, a looming tower himself, a faceless shape in the background of everything. Skin which scratched her cheek when she held him, hands showing how something worked, the weight of a body in a chair. It was seventeen years since he had been a part of her life, and he had faded with the rest of it. She remembered a sense that everything was right, and she knew it existed because someone else arranged the days so invisibly that it seemed these were simply the ways that things happened. She left that behind, too, looming over nothing, to be recovered now only through practice and exercise. It wasn't the same.

She gleaned explanations for some of these things from the knowledge archives beneath the church. The glass towers, she now knew, were built in the last days of the old world in response to rising land costs, presented as icons of prosperity and requisitioned later—after the war—to be repurposed as greenhouses, almost looking like they were built for that task, stealing so much sunlight from the ground on their north sides. The city imported grain but fresh produce was difficult to move, so the south faces of the towers were reinforced to support growing and the lower and northern levels held livestock, compost, and live-in caretakers. The school bus was one of a fleet which moved wealthy children to wherever they would be taught to fit their futures: housekeeping, accountancy and culture for young women; leadership, administration and specialist disciplines for men. There was some crossover among the most gifted in certain niche areas: the state didn't care to regulate the gender of doctors or soldiers or mathematicians, for example, but Holly had never been gifted in that way. As a child she knew only that in her mother's generation women had led, and in hers it was the turn of men, and that was enough to discourage her from competing.

And the dim apartment, which really hadn't been so dim, and the father who really did have a face. They were her home until her mother took her out of the patchwork city and brought her here, supposedly temporarily: the archival church.

She remembered all of the journey. She had never spent so much time with her mother—who, until this journey, worked almost constantly—and without her father. They rode in a borrowed grain truck, her mother at the wheel and she and her sister sharing the other seat. For three days they stopped only to refuel from containers they carried with them and to urinate in the bushes, and Holly refused to do even this until the second day: she was appalled at the idea and threatened to wet herself if her mother refused to find a real toilet, until it because clear that there *was* no real toilet and she finally gave in, crouched awkwardly and refusing her sister's offer to hold her hand, insisting they look elsewhere and, when the moment came, crying as the first splash of waste hit the weeds. Hazel adapted more readily, and their mother had hidden her own feelings. Holly had fought it. She was nine years old. At night they stayed cuddled together against the cold and woke early in all their clothes. Her mother told stories from memory to help them sleep. The days were clear and the road bumped them around and they saw forests, grain farms, brown rivers and miles of hillside. Eventually the air changed and they glimpsed the sea from the windows, and then the church itself: a squat compound high on the hill with allotments stretching down towards the dunes. She had seen it and thought it looked impossibly timid compared to the ancient cathedral she had imagined. The plan had been to stay for a month, initiate the girls into their mother's religion, and return home, but it hadn't worked out that way. Now she knew the church was not empty, and few things surprised her in this place: she had grown to fit it the way one tree grows against another.

Doors didn't lock anywhere in the church, so she didn't think of stalling the record keepers' searches any more than she thought about jumping from the window. Once Lake was gone she had followed his lead and slipped the packet under her clothes, then sat down on the bed. Unlike him, they would let her leave unchecked if she wanted—there was no rule to keep her in the compound. It was impossible to think of anything but the diary next to her belly. She took it out again and set it on her lap.

Her training had prepared her for times like this. She knew how to master her impulses, slow her mind, see herself from outside. This last was what she needed. She breathed. She thought about the situation as if it was happening to someone else. She thought about it as if it was happening to her: as if she was looking forward to it and planning, then back at it and reviewing. She knew she would accept whatever conclusion the thinking presented. She thought about what she would say if her debate with Lake was less urgent. She tried to focus on the question which mattered: what would she have decided to do, if she had already decided? What would she do if neither of their futures depended on it?

The world was still what it was, she would argue. Her job wasn't to want things or change things but to hold things dear, to protect what needed protecting until a place in the world for it opened up again. But people are hurting now, he would answer. There are people outside your church whom you could help. Neither his argument nor her own convinced her. But then she discovered a third voice joining the debate, which she hadn't before known was there. Her other self, she found, didn't share her opinion. It made neither her first suggestion nor his. It said: you would be different if you left.

Her mother had brought her to the church to learn something every prior member of her family had known, and Holly had learned more of the faith than her mother, but she had begun where her mother began: the self-holding exercise of "two selves in one home." The practice maintained separate selves in order to call up and live through whichever was best suited to the moment, and she had continued it out of love despite doubting she would ever again need it. She hadn't envisaged her moments changing again once she accepted a life in the church. But now here it was, her other self, suggesting it might be deserving of this occasion.

It had waited a long time to speak outside of practice, and it had a lot to say. She had to listen carefully—this other self didn't care for discussing ethics, or weighing facts. It didn't much care for breathing exercises. It reminded her a little of being eight years old.

They would come to search her room in the morning.

An image came back to her from nowhere as she struggled to think, clear as any later memory, of her father shouting her name. She could see his face. They stood at opposite ends of a long open hallway, somewhere public, and he was shouting her back. She wanted to press on. She was wearing gloves and the air froze her cheeks. She wanted to go to the city park and she was learning something she didn't yet have a word for: she was learning that, as well as a body and brain and love and desire and discipline, she had something called dignity. She was learning that she now cared about going to the park not only because she wanted to go, but because he was imposing his will to prevent her from going, because he called and expected her to bend to his command. To turn back was an affront to her dignity; to press on was an insult to his, and he would pursue it. He had to pursue it because that was how it worked. They stared each other down and the memory held, and behind him her mother called them both stubborn and strode away, and then with impossible understanding her father laughed and broke the moment, and approached, but she didn't get to remember what he said.

She had kept this self inside her, hidden it away for years while it wasn't welcome in case it might later be needed—just how her faith worked, and just how her mother had planned, and almost as if her mother had been right. It said it was needed now. Its fire was licking up into new flames. It said it knew what to do. She thought about her mother. She thought what she would think. She thought, how strange, to now be granted a real memory of my father. To remember what the world felt like, when I was only a beginning.

Memory works in the telling, and what you choose to tell becomes what happened. What you did, why it mattered, what it means: memory makes it.

She looked at the packet in her lap, and at the door, and folded her hands.

The Last Outpost

by David England

"I don't think they're coming, sir." Shelley's voice was steady, betraying none of the anxiety I knew she was feeling. Hazel eyes held mine briefly from beneath an auburn mane pulled back into the severe bun required for long hair in low-grav. She was the youngest of our group—twenty-seven, bright-eyed, and a bit over-eager. But the kid knew her stuff and could hotwire a failing com system with the code-jockey equivalent of a paperclip and a wad of used chewing gum. I could respect that.

I nodded to her and looked around at the others. All five of us, the entire crew of of the lunar station *Selene*, were clustered around the table in the small briefing room that tripled as our mess hall and rec space.

"Gil." I turned. Stan Carter was a burly man with that middle-age salt-and-pepper look so many of us guys get. We had a low-tension rivalry, Stan and I. Both experienced engineers, both with the chops afforded by career and age—he was only a year older at forty-seven. But the difference between us was that his degree was from Georgia Tech and mine Annapolis. So he was mission engineer for Diana 13 and I was in the command slot. And if this little party of ours wasn't a Marine's billet, I don't know what would be. *Situation Normal—All Fucked Up.* Hoo-yah.

"Yes, Stan?"

"She's right. They're not coming for us. The launch schedule was for six days ago. Three days' transit. We've seen no launch, tracked no signal. We've done nothing but eat their static for weeks."

He was right, too. The retrieval craft was a good three days overdue. And we'd have been able to track its journey the whole way in. So far—nothing. We'd discussed the possibilities when radio contact first began getting sporadic in the last month and a half, before it fell into the void completely. Nineteen days ago. Not that I was counting.

Stan continued. "Like I've been saying since things first got screwy, we need to look at the evac protocol. That's our only way off this rock. We're on our own here."

"We've talked about this already," I responded, keeping my temper tamped down good and tight. "The evac protocol only takes us to HEO. We need ground-control guidance through the lower-orbit debris fields in order to land and we have no idea if anyone is even manning the line on the other end. The pod carries four days' environmental for a full crew. I don't want to die a slow death in orbit. We've got ample enviro here. We can afford to wait and establish a com link before we launch."

"And what if no one's listening?" Stan countered. "What if the situation is only going from bad to worse down there? The longer we wait, the more things have a chance to unravel. High earth orbit wasn't part of the original protocol— you know that. The evac-to-ground programming is still in the manual. Even Jensen here could reset it."

I cast a quick glance at William Jensen, the station science lead. An astronomer by training, he was a quiet one. A thin man of thirty-eight, he had a pinched face and prematurely thinning hair. Jensen said nothing and I turned my attention back to Stan.

"If it comes down to rolling the dice and flying through the debris field blind, we'll do it. But not until our other options are crossed off. We have time. Let's keep our heads and use our resources. Doc—" I addressed the last member of our group, "what's your best estimate of our environmental capabilities?"

"Doc" was Carla Liebowitz, our mission medical officer. She was also the oldest at fifty-two, with steel-grey hair and the beginnings of those sage-like wrinkle lines associated with wise grandmothers, although her more choice language made one think of drunken sailors in a friendly dispute. She brooked no nonsense and told it straight. I liked her.

"That depends on what you're looking for. Stan's checked the power and heating systems. The batteries and solar panels are in excellent shape. We've got good water and atmospheric recycling. In a pinch, we could supplement water or oxygen losses by mining some of the ice deposits in Shackleton crater. Food is our major concern. Standard planning overage gives us an additional month beyond schedule at normal consumption. We're a half a week into that already, but we can stretch it out by skimping a bit. Then, of course, there's the garden."

I nodded at that. The station's hydroponic system was constructed as a psychological buffer for the crew against the starkness of long-term lunar living—a bit of greenery goes a long way toward soothing the nerves—and also served as a secondary CO_2 scrubber. The medical officer of Diana ɪɪ had caused a minor uproar back on Earth when she smuggled heirloom seeds onboard in her personal gear and proceeded to establish a non-GMO vegetable garden, displacing a good bit of the designer-gene foliage that had been contracted for the station. Carla's immediate predecessor had completed the work, removing the last of the original plants.

"If we work in more of the produce from the garden," Carla continued, "we can extend our food supply a good ways—*quite* a good ways if you don't mind eating a lot of salads and beans. We are going to run out of coffee at some point, though. I can't do anything about that." She smiled wryly, with that sardonic gleam in her eye we'd all come to know.

"I'm not sitting on this lump of rock for another month," Stan interjected. "I say we go now."

Shelley spoke up. "The commander's right. We need to see if we can link up with ground before we evac."

"Hey, Space Cadet," Stan snapped at her, "drop the whole chain-of-command shtick, okay? We're all equally screwed on this rig. And it's not like we all don't know that you've had the hots for our Lord and Master here since the first day of training."

Shelley blushed furiously and looked down at her feet. I fought to keep my temper in check.

"Stow that shit right now, Carter." My jaw clenched. "We're going to keep it together and work this problem. But this ain't no democracy and if you don't care for that reality then you know where the airlock is. Don't make me throw you in it. Capisce?"

Stan grunted sullenly, but gave a curt nod.

"Alright." I looked around at everyone. "This is what we're going to do. First, Shelley's going to keep working the com. Scan frequencies, search alternate channels, hack satellites—whatever you can dream up, try it." Shelley nodded, giving me a wavering smile of thanks.

I continued. "Second, we're going to prep for the long haul. That means pulling in the food that's cached at the observatory in Shackleton. We'll do a standard excursion—Stan and Jensen will go out; I'll be on stand-by; and Doc'll monitor everyone's vitals from here. Shelley will keep at her other job."

"Third, we're going to get through this. But we've got to keep our heads on straight."

"Sounds like a plan," Carla commented. "And not half-bad given that it's freshly pulled out of your ass."

I smiled tightly. "Some of my best plans come from there." I leaned back in my chair. "Okay, people. We've got a long day ahead tomorrow, so I want everyone to get a solid eight. Next watch rotation," I glanced over at the schedule, "has me up first, then Stan. Jensen's on swing. Shelley's got the crap watch, and Doc finishes up. Any questions?" Seeing none: "You all hit the racks then. I'll be upstairs."

Our little group broke apart, each heading to his or her quarters. Carla hung back momentarily. Placing a hand on my arm, she cocked her head slightly and just looked at me for a good minute before giving what I could only take as a nod of approval. As she, too, left the room, I let out a long breath.

Well, it was no St. Crispin's Day speech, that's for damn sure. But then I'm no Henry the Fifth, either. Just another grunt dropped into a pile of shit, scrambling to stay alive for a bit longer. I swung through the hatch. Catching a rung, I climbed up to the CIC for my watch.

Slipping into the seat at my command console, I looked over the snug space that was the coordinated information center, the hub of our little outfit. Communications and engineering were situated ahead and slightly below me, with science and medical behind and slightly above. Most of Jensen's (and a good portion of Doc's) work was done in dedicated facilities elsewhere in the station, but these were useful for excursions and other coordinated work. A large and very thick window filled the curved front wall, offering a panoramic lunar view. Walkways along either side of the CIC led down to a narrow observation platform for anyone who wanted a better look. I could see just fine from where I sat.

The Diana program was to have been America's triumphant return to the moon. "Reclaiming the nation's rightful place," as some had intoned. Initially developed under the preceding administration, it had been rechristened and fast-tracked when the current President made her historic win in the '28 election. One of those scions of political dynasty, a sense of vindication permeated her inaugural address. Symbolism is important to people like that. So "Constellation" became "Diana." I didn't care what the top brass called the damn thing—we were going back to the moon.

The first Diana missions were the usual orbital testing of the new vehicle designs, Constellation 1 and Constellation 2 having been quietly and retroactively renamed. Diana 5 was the much-celebrated flag-planting ceremony, where we once again touched lunar soil. The President's rhetoric soared to new heights and she vowed that we were there to stay. The next pair of missions—executed nearly in parallel—were polar scouting expeditions to determine America's next bold step: the establishment of a permanent lunar station.

After a brief but spirited debate in the press, the southern pole was chosen and our site at Malepar Mountain—with its favorable line-of-sight to earth and ready access to sunlight for power—was selected. Follow-on missions built the station and the enormous radio telescope at nearby Shackleton crater, the human crews overseeing the work done by a small army of semi-autonomous construction 'bots. With much fanfare, the station crew of Diana 11 took up residence on October 23, 2032. The President was re-elected in a landslide that just fell short of Reagan's some forty

-eight years earlier. Her second inaugural rose even higher than her first, laying out a vision for America's "irrevocable mantle of leadership" in humanity's conquest of space.

My wife Karen, on the other hand, had never been keen on the space program or my place in it. "Why can we send people to the moon," she'd ask, "but not have roads without potholes or bridges that don't collapse?" But seeing that it both paid the bills and kept her husband happy, she managed to tolerate it well enough.

She voiced strong disapproval, though, when my number came up for Diana 13. I pointed out that the Apollo mission had turned out okay in the end, to be rewarded with one of those *we are not amused* looks I'd come to know quite well in the course of two decades of marriage. Given the mission schedule and its fourteen-month commitment—three months for pre-mission training, ten months on-site, and a month's debrief and rehabilitation—I'd be starting only weeks after our twenty-third anniversary and would completely miss the twenty-fourth. I promised her that our silver anniversary would be a blow-out.

The children, now young adults themselves, were excited for me. Robbie (that is, Robert Giles Sullivan, Jr.) had popped into the world nine months to the day after our wedding, prompting our families to rib us mercilessly about not even being able to wait until the honeymoon. Karen and I would laugh along with the joke, casting knowing looks at each other and relishing the shared memory of a certain storage room and fifteen stolen minutes at our reception. Samantha Rose followed her brother eighteen months later. Both grew up NASA kids, fully immersed in the program. That their dad was going to the moon was as natural as the sun rising in the morning.

So the universe narrowed as my crew began training together, gradually excluding much of the external world. After the first month of pre-mission training, we went into continuous confinement, learning the fine art of living together in close quarters. At that point, our only contact with the outside was via com link. I'd spotted Shelley's behavior right away—it's the sort of thing any commander needs to keep an eye out for when leading a mixed-gender team—and made sure that she was on the far side of me in the watch rotation we'd be using. Finagling the assignment of quarters to situate us on opposite ends was added insurance. She was a good kid who showed a lot of promise—it would have been a shame for her to have been bumped for something like that.

As the rest of the world faded and the mission increasingly became our sole focus, only bits and pieces of news would make it onto our radar. The long-running intervention in Venezuela, entering its ninth year, had taken a sharp turn for the worse. Shortly before our launch date, the President had executed one of those "we're leaving because we want to, not because you made us" maneuvers in an attempt to save face and money. It didn't work. We were halfway to the moon when the stock market crashed, rolled over, and just plain died.

It was less than three months into our stint that the first rumors of serious domestic troubles filtered through. The National Guard being sent into this or that city to put down a riot was nothing new, but this felt different. It was like one of those old whack-a-mole games from my grandfather's day—every time the military went in, the trouble would tuck away and pop up somewhere else. Then one mole became two, and two moles became three. I could see the all-too-familiar pattern that was developing and where that particular trail led frankly scared the shit of of me.

I started putting out feelers for early retrieval then—quietly, when I was alone on my watch—only to get the run-around. Four months later, a chunk of the Louisiana Guard that had been activated to fight the insurgents—what else am I supposed to call them?—disappeared into the bayous, taking their weapons with them. When most of the Idaho Guard went over to the fighters holed up in the Bitterroots a week after that, I stopped pussy-footing around.

"Steve," I said to the mission director, "we need evac and we need it now. You and I both know the shit's hitting the fan down there. I need to get my people home." I had the swing watch that night and we'd switched over to a private channel so that we could talk plainly.

"Gil, I copy what you're saying, but no-can-do for early pick-up." Steve's voice was even. "Orders from the top. *The* top, if you understand my meaning. 'The schedule will not be altered.' That's a direct quote. You'll be picked up when your shift is done. "

"You're *not* going to be sending another crew to rotate in after us. Tell me she's not that stupid."

Steve coughed. "I didn't copy that last part, Gil. No, not on my watch. I'm making that as plain as I can on this end. But there's no budging the schedule for you guys." "Irrevocable mantle" and all that, I thought. "Those are the orders."

Orders. I'd clutched at that straw when the com link began getting spotty and held it tightly in my fist when the radio went silent. A Marine follows orders. A Marine also leaves no one behind. Presidents operate differently, it would seem.

A not-terribly-subtle clearing of the throat brought me back to the present. Stan gave me a cursory nod as he settled into his station and took over the watch. I climbed down the hatch and headed to my quarters for some much-needed shut-eye.

The blaring of the alarm jerked me awake. My eyes snapped to the wall terminal, whose read-out told the stark truth: the evac pod was being activated.

Swearing, I hurled myself through the hatch as it was still opening and immediately collided with another body hurtling down the corridor. I blinked as I realized it was Stan.

"It's Jensen!" he shouted over the wail as we disentangled ourselves from each other. "He's in the pod!"

We flew along the passageway, throwing ourselves from one grab-bar to another. The evacuation hatch came into view and my heart dropped as I saw that the blast shield behind it had already been sealed.

"The override!" I yelled and flung myself at the panel beside the hatch. But even as I flipped up the cover to punch in my authorization code, the station shuddered. I clung to a nearby grab-bar as our only remaining way home launched into space.

The shaking faded away. Reflexively, I hit the button to silence the alarm. A terrible quiet descended. Then the left side of my face exploded in pain, the force of the blow hurling me against the far wall of the corridor.

"*You stupid fucker!*" Stan screamed, his face ugly with fury. His fist was already drawing back as he advanced. My vision partially blurred, I could make out the others behind him. Shelley's eyes were wide, a long braid still falling slowly over her shoulder. Carla's expression was grim, her jaw set.

"You wouldn't listen to me and now we're all fucked! I'm going to fucking kill y— Gah!" His rant cut off in a sudden cry, a startled look replacing the rage. He twisted awkwardly to look behind him and as he did so, I spotted a small dart protruding from his back, just under his left shoulder blade.

"You bi . . ." Stan's expletive faded into silence as he slumped to the floor.

I looked up. The tableau was frozen in surreality. Stan's crumpled form. Shelley's mouth open, her lips forming a small "o." Carla's eyes hard, her arm still extended with an odd-looking pistol in her grip.

"I don't mean to sound ungrateful, Doc," I said, attempting to regain my composure. "But what the hell are you doing with a weapon?"

"I'll explain in a minute," she replied, bending over Stan and removing the dart with a sharp tug. "First, you and Shelley help me get him to medical." Shelley came forward and the three of us maneuvered Stan down the passage to sick bay. Carla opened the hatchway and we settled him on one of the beds. After she had strapped him in and given him a good looking-over, I spoke up.

"Alright, Doc. Now."

Carla stood and faced me squarely. "Emergency medical protocol 1273-A authorizes the medical officer to utilize forced sedation in the event of violent psychological breakdown by a member of the crew."

"Bullshit, Carla. There's no such protocol."

"It's a restricted protocol. Medical officer only."

"And exactly when was I to be told about this?"

Carla quoted again. "Medical officer is directed to reveal the existence of the protocol and an outline of its parameters to the effective commander of the station immediately upon execution. Consider yourself duly notified, Gil."

"'Effective commander'?" I asked, puzzled.

"A contingency, of course. The commander might be the one who snaps. Wasn't in this case. Stan had been exhibiting preliminary stressors for a while now, but things ramped up only very recently. After yesterday's little show, I'd figured he was going to pop soon. And I was so focused on him that Jensen slipped right under my nose. In short, Skipper, I fucked up royally."

"No one saw that coming." I attempted to clear my head by shaking it, still trying to absorb what had been thrown at me, and failed miserably on both counts. Something was different with Carla; I couldn't put my finger on it. "But tell me again why it is that the medical officer is the one holding the keys here?"

"We're deemed the most stable of the crew and the least likely to suffer a breakdown. Mission medical personnel undergo rigorous psychological screening."

"We're all screened—" Carla cut off my protest with a wave of her hand.

"*Rigorous* psychological screening," she repeated, and gave a tight smile. "How do I put this succinctly? All of us had shrinks crawl around inside our heads, okay? But with me, they went in through my ass."

I looked at her blankly, totally at a loss for words.

"Now," she directed. "You and Shelley go put some ice on that face of yours. That'll hold the swelling down—aside from some bruising, you're going to live. I'll be with you two in a few minutes."

Still a bit dazed and my face throbbing, I swung through the hatch into the briefing room and slid into my customary seat. Shelley came in right after, her braid trailing behind. She passed me without comment and went straight to the kitchenette.

I just stared at the table, trying to process all that had just happened. Shelley appeared at my side, pressing a towel-encased ice-pack into my hand and holding it to my face. "You've got to put this on your eye, Gil," she urged softly. "Doc said."

As if invoked, Carla materialized in the hatchway. "I'm not one for long speeches, so I'll keep this short and sweet." It was then that I realized that the familiar glint in her eye was gone. "I gave Stan something to put him to sleep. It—seemed the best option under the circumstances." A pregnant silence filled the space. "As for me, I think I'll suit up and go for a nice, long walk. Maybe do some sight-seeing. There's food in the fridge." She paused, looking at me pointedly. "You kids don't wait up for me." Her eyes held mine until I gave her a curt nod. Then she was gone.

I stared at the open hatchway for what seemed like an eternity, then watched as the indicators on the wall terminal showed the cycling of the airlock.

The relentless, mocking beat of my own heart pounded in my ears. Frustration boiled over and I surged to my feet, hurling the ice-pack across the room. It struck the far wall with a muffled but satisfying crunch. Saying nothing, I left and hauled my useless carcass up to the CIC.

Ignoring my station, I went down front to the observation platform. My hands gripped the low railing under the window, a gaping void opening in my chest. I looked out over the barren, grey landscape, then lifted my gaze beyond to where that beautifully-misted blue-and-green ball hung in the dark tapestry of the lunar sky. Karen. Robbie. Sam.

Karen.

There was movement in the corner of my vision as a billowing cloud of dark fire settled next to me. Warm, slender fingers touched my hand, tentatively at first, before entwining themselves with my own. After a moment's hesitation, I responded with a gentle squeeze. We stayed that way for a long time.

The Last of His Kind

by Hannes Rollin

Twilight came. The wallpaper crackled in the icy air. I sensed grotesque shadows prowling the expanses of my office like a beast straight out of a Lovecraft tale. Of course, my nerves were on edge. Too many things had happened that should never have happened. My gaze switched between the two men before me and the little laptop they had brought with them. It was a beauty, made from a massive chunk of aluminum gleaming ominously in the candlelight, running a brisk processor, a silent hard drive, and a bunch of other gizmos no one understood, but everyone wanted. Too bad those weren't made anymore.

"Gentlemen, shall we start?" I asked. I hadn't invited them. Not that I didn't need help—I didn't like their philosophy. It was stupid and wrong. The whole procedure would be nothing but painful. Still, I had no choice. I didn't dare to think what would happen next, as our generators churned away the last drops of diesel.

"Sure. Let's. Thanks for having us here, Mr. Hamilton," said Asterix, small and lean and agile even when sitting still. He wore a shirt with a Buddhist symbol.

The two had given me their names, Smiths both, but they reminded me so much of those old French comic heroes that I allowed myself the liberty to call them Asterix and Obelix, inwardly.

"I see you have a long list, and so do we," Asterix said, and stretched his back in a cat-like gesture, quickly shaking his head awake. Obelix grunted something under his breath.

"At any rate, thanks for coming. I didn't expect you to care for such an out-of-the-way hospital like ours," I said.

"Oh, well. The PG sees to it that the circulation remains centralized, but that doesn't mean we leave the limps dying. Did you expect us to sit on our hands while our young country goes to pieces?"

The Provisional Government. They were indeed busy keeping things going despite electricity being down, internet down, long-distance trade down, gasoline coming in intermittent trickles. The PG had seized all real estate, manufacturing, IT. Rumors had it they ransacked a fair number of survivalist shelters to equip the new police. To be fair, they got fresh water running and landlines working in some places. Here in the clinic, we had done our best eating up our reserves, but now we were almost down. My head spun with the list of interconnected and mutually reinforcing problems as soon as I started thinking about them. It was all much more than I could hold in mind at once. For better or worse.

I sighed a bit too loud and said, "Sit on your hands? Yes. No. I don't know. Most of us think it's a temporary condition. Myself, I've already made my peace with the end of the world. I'm only here out of an irrational sense of duty, I suspect." I tried to smile, but the result was probably pathetic.

"End of the world? Oh my," said Asterix, who did all the talking. Obelix just chuckled. "Every end is a new beginning, Mr. Hamilton, and we're working hard to get as much blessing as possible out of the curse the old times made for us. No, the world may be old, but it's far from ending."

"Speaking of the old times," I said, "do you know how things are in the Middle East?" I thought of my van sitting in the parking outside, useless. Since Texas had gone the other way, I had to walk to my office. And the lack of internet and television had left ample room for speculation. Maybe someday soon the Middle East oil would flow again. Maybe the situation was indeed temporary, after all. Wait another month, officials had proclaimed, and another month. Maybe.

"It was *such* a stupid idea to duke it out in Arabia," said Asterix. "The country is on fire, and that's not a metaphor. The Saud family lives in tents—that is, those who still live. The Chinese are all over the place. The Middle East is a matter of the past. They're going medieval faster than Jim Kunstler could spell 'misallocation of resources.' Forget the Middle East. Now's the time to clean our own house. There will be some fuel, some electricity, but it won't be much. We don't know the details."

"Fair enough," I said with a raspy voice. "Let's get down to it. The first item on my list: We can't handle the current number of patients. They're too many."

"Do you have precise figures?" Asterix asked. "Statistics of the past months, showing patients per department, length of stay, grouped by condition, staff statistics, etcetera?"

"Yes," I said, fumbling with the stack of paper on my desk until I got the folder. Some of the very last printouts, strewn with handwritten updates. I gave it to Asterix, who gave it to Obelix without looking at it. The question marks must have been all over my face.

Asterix said, "We'll have to change the clinic. John will write a program to find the optimum sequence of actions."

Obelix stroked his ponytail while skimming the abstract; then he started typing the numbers into the laptop, his large hands moving with the fluidity of an expert pianist. I'm not sure how he managed not to hit two keys at once. He was clad all in black but still looked fat.

"I'll have to fire people?" I said, expecting the worst.

"No, quite the contrary. You'll have to admit much fewer patients, though. And most of the nurses and doctors will be asked to join the GMS on occasion."

"What on earth is that?"

"General Medical Service. You don't need a neurosurgeon to prescribe rest and herbal tea. For many minor illnesses, it's better for you not to come out here, so the medic comes to you. The system will be set up as a rotating duty."

"And who pays for that?" I asked. Preposterous.

"Why, the PG." Asterix flashed an elvish smile as if I hadn't gotten the joke yet. That moment, Obelix stopped typing and pressed a single button with intent. For a few seconds, nothing happened. Then, the laptop made a gentle chime. Asterix and Obelix lowered their heads over the tiny screen, exchanging a few technical terms in low voices. I overheard something about optimization or combinatorics; I didn't understand a thing. Obelix copied words and numbers off the screen, writing with a tiny pencil. I wanted to ask something, but Asterix hushed me with a gesture of his hand. After a minute or two, Obelix had finished and gave me the sheet, which was full of words and numbers in a careless crawl.

I held the paper closer to the candle on my desk. *Departments to be closed*, I read, not quite believing my eyes. Then a bland list with dates. *Departments to be merged. Personnel for General Medical Service, in percent.* More numbers. Big ones.

With an effort, I lifted my eyes and glanced at the two men. "Next point?" said Asterix with a maddening cheerfulness.

"We're low on food," I said, feeling the cold creeping up my legs. "Especially dairies, meat, coffee. No cooking without electricity."

"At least you have your hospital kitchen," Asterix said. "Otherwise, you would've had to set one up, transportation being what it is. Okay," he interrupted himself, "people get used to living without coffee in a matter of a few days. Getting back to naps and walks and rosemary tea takes considerably longer. Probably you didn't notice, but the new departments will be a bit overstaffed. We'll fix shift schedules so that there's leeway for unanticipated sick leaves, holidays, redirections, GMS, and the like."

"That's good news," I said. "Overstaffed and underfed." Might be that I didn't even sound cynical.

"Now, now," Asterix said. "First of all, the PG encourages vegetarian food." He smirked. "It goes easier on the economy. We've worked out fully functional menus, raw food, regional and all. Besides, stochastic fasting is the best medicine."

"Forgive me if I call that an egregious proposition," I answered. I shot a glance at Obelix. You couldn't attain such a figure as a vegetarian ascetic. Something was deeply wrong here. "Next point," I said with an effort. "Heating. Thank God spring is coming."

"Yes," said Asterix. "Because of the restructuring, half of your rooms will be vacant, reducing hospital activities to the lower floors. You wouldn't waste what little electricity you got on elevators. And your people will have to carry a few tons of dirt into the clinic."

"Dirt? What for?"

"For the ovens. A well-built clay oven heats a big area for a night and a day with an armful of wood. Decentralization is the order of the day. We have optimized the oven design." He nodded at Obelix. "It takes a day to learn how to build one. You can extract the clay when you dig up your pretty lawns."

My amazement must have shown all too clearly, as Asterix and Obelix gave me a paternal you-still-don't-get-it smile. "Gardens," said Asterix. "Did you think the PG keeps tossing bread from army trucks forever?"

"No. I'm surprised they did it in the first place after all the imports stopped and combines were left to collect rust and looters were shot on sight."

"Wheat storage in undisclosed locations. Good thing in times like these."

"Sure," I said, thinking of the lunch I'd skipped. "Next point: We're low on anesthetics. Imagine operating without anesthetics. Also, painkillers, tranquilizers, antibiotics, disinfectants, you name it. The list is longer than the good old tax code."

"Oh, interesting topic." Asterix rubbed his forehead. It was a game to him, an exercise in problem-solving. He didn't take any of this seriously. He continued in his quick way. "We're negotiating with our new neighbors to get basic supplies, but it won't be much. You'll cope with less. For once, don't waste anesthetics for minor operations. Use hypnosis if you can."

"What?"

"A third of the population can be easily hypnotized, another third so-so, the rest not at all. So, you can do roughly half of the operations without chemistry."

"How long does it take to learn hypnosis?" I said.

"Essentially, a couple of days. Hypnosis is embarrassingly easy. The difficult point is to look trustworthy and authoritative, but that's what medical school is for." He chuckled.

I had heard about hypnosis from my dentist but didn't take it seriously then. It sounded too easy to be worthwhile. "Why didn't we do it earlier?" I asked. "Wasn't it scientifically proven?"

"It was. It's only that the old times always looked for the biggest profits, and those can't be had with hypnosis. Profits mean taxes, jobs, more taxes, hence more government handouts, more voters, more taxes. You get the picture. So, the government played along, and a lot of fascinating studies got shoved into the archives. But times are changing. What's next?"

"The second half of the operations," I reminded him grimly.

"Reduce them," Asterix said, and shrugged.

"*Reduce them?*" I said, almost screaming. "You say I should let all those people suffer and die?"

"No, Mr. Hamilton, of course not," Asterix said. Obelix scribbled something and handed me the paper. I deciphered the names of the most frequent operations with their numbers. To the right were negative percentages, more numbers, sums. It didn't quite make sense.

"Then what?" I said.

"Take the C-section," Asterix said. "What's the quote?" he asked.

"Twenty-five percent," Obelix said without looking up.

"That's not too bad. You can, pardon, cut the rate to ten percent by observing a few simple rules. Say, leaving out the doctor until the midwife calls him of her own—"

"Not in your—" I interrupted him, but Asterix interrupted me in turn: "Oh yes, we have the studies. Ten percent isn't an average; it's the maximum." He gave me a lurid brochure.

"I'm astonished that the PG has the means to conduct studies," I said.

"It hasn't," said Asterix. "We took out old studies and read them with new eyes. Maximum effect by energy expenditure, factoring in education, transport, and pollution. The obvious. Things are tight, you know."

My ears reddened.

"Many births are already happening at home," Asterix said, "and that's as it should be. Once your medical staff is re-educated, C-section rate will drop below five percent. Same with appendicitis. Doesn't even need to be operated in many cases."

"Re-educated?" I asked.

"Homeopathy and acupuncture. Three months each, full time."

"Frankly, that's bogus," I said, but my comment only earned me that paternal look again. "The whole alternative medicine scheme is outrageously *unscientific*," I said with a violent hiss.

"You'll change your mind once you see birth labors starting the instant a little needle gets pricked into the woman's toe, or once you see heavy pneumonia subside on a single dose of something that has nothing in it." He grinned at me.

For a change, Obelix added in a voice fitting his figure, "Nothing, that is, besides information." He patted his shiny laptop. "You can do a lot with the right information at the right place."

I could only shake my head in disbelief. The interview got worse and worse. "Homeopathy? Spare me. That's impossible. Suggestion and placebo effect," I said.

"No matter how many studies you produce. It's impossible." My voice didn't sound like my own anymore.

Asterix inclined his head and studied me for a few seconds. "You don't need to do that. We know others are waiting their turn. Besides," he said, then yawned before he continued, "did you know that nineteenth century homeopaths invented the controlled double-blind study? And did you know how many lives homeopaths saved during the Spanish flu in 1918? The numbers are mind-boggling. And big pharma never found a chemical compound against influenza that wasn't worse than the flu, anyway."

That hurt. "Alright, alright," I said, ignoring the buzz in my head, "let's go on. Intercom. Bad things are happening, and precious resources are being wasted because information flows are too slow."

"Simple thing," Asterix said. "Get runners. Boys and girls carrying messages here"—he pointed at his head—"and using these"—he tapped on his legs. "John will compute the number of runners you'll need, the optimum locations for bulletin boards, and a schedule." Obelix was already typing as Asterix continued, "You may not know it yet. The PG will issue a bill next week, closing some schools, releasing older students, abolishing compulsory attendance. There'll be plenty of young people to choose from."

"Uh," I said. Runners. Ovens. Gardens on the hospital lawn. It seemed the PG wanted to follow the Middle East back to the middle ages. "One more thing," I said. "Salary. I lost a significant number of employees since we stopped paying them."

"Yes, we thought about that. You'll have to make do until April somehow. Then the new currency comes out. No electronic payments anymore, just beautiful little banknotes and checks. They come in different colors. You won't like this, but your salary will be the same as everyone else's, from surgeon to orderly. It simplifies a lot of things. But you *will* get a salary, and you *will* be able to buy things, which is a lot less self-evident than you might think."

Ouch, I thought, ouch, ouch, ouch. "Reminds me of something Karl Marx wrote," I said, trying to look sinister.

"That has nothing to do with Marx," Asterix said. "The income spread of the old times was an *anomaly*. It was a feature of a system that was apt to break its neck by design. It couldn't last, and so it didn't. Look around," he said, pointing at the palm trees at the shadowy back of my office, at my library of medical classics and legal references, at my chesterfield. "You're hugely privileged by the power you wield and by the convenience of your life. Think of Saudi princes having teatime sitting on the fine sands of their grandfathers. Think of the people of Venezuela who get what they eat from the jungle, if at all. Think of the expecting mothers out there sleeping in cardboard huts. And still, you want to get paid extra for your privileges?"

I let out a puff of air that formed an eerie cloud; illumined by the candle, it looked nothing like ectoplasm. I didn't know what to answer. I wanted to say something about responsibility and representativeness, but a half-conscious nagging thought prevented me. These guys wouldn't understand. They had a mindset that dealt with caveats like Mike Tyson with opponents half his weight. Why hurt myself anymore? Why subject myself to any more of this nonsense?

"One last item before I go out and drown myself in the garden pond," I said. "Mental cases. Our psychiatrists were the first to run out of medication. They started locking people up or sending them home, according to the condition."

"Ah, that one." Asterix wiggled his head in a funny motion. "Re-education includes a few weeks of energy healing, which deals with most of the issues. The rest . . ." He made an innocent gesture. "Case by case."

I gasped. "You want me to lead a bunch of exorcists? Are you insane?"

"You don't know the first thing, do you?" asked Asterix. He sat up straight and looked at my chest, slowly moving his hand, palm facing outwards. I felt a pressure on my heart. An illusion, I thought. No. Hypnosis. Nothing wrong; I'm not suggestible. But the pressure didn't subside. It got worse. After a few moments, I discovered that I was nearly paralyzed and could hardly breathe.

"Would . . . you . . . please . . ." I said, holding my heart, staring at him. Asterix made a few quick motions with his hand, and the pressure was gone as if he had just taken a ton of lead off me. Crazy. My pulse hammered in my temples.

"Now, normally I don't do the show, but you're exceptionally stubborn," he said, and shrugged. He then closed his eyes and breathed curiously. I felt my shoulders relax. After a time, the rest of me relaxed as well. These guys were idiots, sure, probably self-employed bloggers dabbling in conspiracy theories in the old times, but they had that kind of flawless logic that could nail you fixed; I was enough of a technocrat to appreciate that. But if their conclusions led to something other than the truth, there must have been a problem with their premises. Without quite noticing how I got there, I found myself smiling. Asterix opened his eyes again and grinned. An odd noise escaped my throat, half blubbering and half giggling; a moment later I was laughing uncontrollably about the silliness of it all. It was so funny. It was all so hilariously mad that I knew nothing else to do but laughing, laughing, laughing, until my sides hurt and my voice failed for want of air and my vision blurred behind a profusion of tears. Then I lost it. From one second to the next I slipped into blackness as if someone had just turned off my brain.

However, a flicker of consciousness remained. Beyond the outer darkness that surrounded me, I heard the muffled basso of Obelix, weirdly distorted.

"What a waste. I told you we've got to replace all key figures with good folks. The old ones are senile. They can't adapt."

"Yeah, right. But at least we tried," Asterix said. And then, after a pause: "How long do you think will he last in the fields?"

In the Court of the Kazakhs

by Jeanne Labonte

BISHOP MATTEO DIPIETRO SAT ON THE HARD WOODEN BENCH, grateful for the thick cushion under his rump, while the Kazakh song-priest regaled his audience with one of their long historical ballads detailing their migration from the war-blasted plains of their forebears to their current home. He suspected many of the Ukraini whose ancestors had fled north and west before the Kazakh onslaught in the early twenty-third century would take great exception to the depiction of their former homeland as being empty and waiting for inhabitants. He dipped his pen into his inkpot, refreshing it while the song-priest paused briefly. The Kazakhian mullah sitting next to him, Tokbolat Smagulov, leaned over and whispered, "You don't need to write down everything he sings. We have manuscripts of the ancient histories of our people."

Matteo chuckled "Really? I thought your song-priests got terribly upset at the idea of having their history ballads written down."

"Well, they do put up a bit of fuss," smiled Tokbolat. "They acknowledge the value of writing for preserving knowledge. Their position is that the histories have more vigor and greater fidelity when told orally. It's an old argument. It will probably still be going on long after you and I are gone."

"Well, actually I'm just writing about the court. Almost none of my people have ever been here, at least not as freemen. I'm trying to document what people are wearing." Matteo sighed regretfully. "But I'm not a very good artist, so I must write it all down. I can't remember the last time I saw so many different styles and colors in one place. And so many dancers! I'm not sure I'll be able to describe it all. Your people are putting on a wonderful celebration."

"Well, we do love our traditions. It is what has kept us strong for so long."

"Does the Khan always wear such an elaborate costume? It's twice as big as he is.

He looks so uncomfortable."

That was putting it mildly. The Khan, leader of the Great Zhuz, resembled an overdressed child's doll, swaddled in furred robes embroidered with rich curling designs and a scarlet cap sporting folds faintly reminiscent of Matteo's own bishop's miter, with the addition of fur trimming the brim and a miniature tower encrusted with jewels jutting up nearly thirty centimeters from the center of the headdress. In reality, the aged Arystanbek was a huge man who made the short stout Matteo feel like a dwarf when he had first been presented to him as a visitor to the court.

"Rumor says he hasn't been well for some time," replied Tokbolat. "But you're right; those garments make him look like he has shrunk. However, with today the beginning of New Day, our New Year celebrations, everyone has to get dressed up."

Khan's three young sons sat near him. The heir-presumptive, Bekzat, sat beside his father, a little higher than his two younger brothers, Nurlan and Kirill. Wearing their own elaborate robes and headdresses, all three were robust copies of their formidable sire.

Discreet contacts between Kazakh and Church scholars over the years after the current Khan assumed power had enabled Matteo to become fluent in their language, and now listening closely to the gossip flowing through the court, he learned that the two younger men were highly ambitious and thought sure to challenge their brother once the elder Khan passed away. Matteo watched them fidget while the song-priest droned on.

As he wiped perspiration from his balding forehead, another member of the audience caught his attention. Seated on the other side of the royal yurt was the grim figure of Ruslan Yussupov, clad almost entirely in plain black except for a broad red sash around his waist. The gaunt, bent, grey-haired man, with his distinctive Zlavic features and watery blue eyes protruding like a frog's, glared in arrogance about him, while a young mahogany skinned man, a slave, held books and wrote quickly whenever Yussupov spoke to him. While his occupation was that of a scrap metal merchant and blacksmith, Ruslan's whispered reputation as a sorcerer ensured the people sitting around him kept a significant distance from him. Matteo suspected the reputation arose from Ruslan's metal forging abilities. He had seen the scarecrow-like figure hammering away in a forge located near the court grounds, a sign of his favored status. Among his most notable creations was a gun which fired pebbles using gunpowder he had concocted himself. He fiercely guarded the secret to its formula and used it as a lever to enhance his position in the hopes of getting into the royal court.

The existence of any sort of gunpowder here among the Kazakhs was alarming, though Matteo reflected that Ruslan's possessiveness kept the knowledge of its making from spreading, at least so far. But he harbored no illusions about that always remaining the case. In previous centuries, the loss of gunpowder among the eastern barbarians ensured that their occasional raids into western Europe, the last one occurring during Matteo's boyhood, could be beaten back by the cannons and firearms still used by the patchwork clusters of countries, tattered remnants of the ancient nations once so powerful. The last forty years of peace had in large measure been due to the iron rule of the Khan, who preferred expending his energies in combat with the Zlavs, Govinas, Belrooz and other tribal groups, many of them descendants of the refugee migrations of earlier centuries who persistently intruded into the lands the Kazakhs had claimed for their own. How long this balance would be maintained once gunpowder reemerged was anyone's guess.

The sound of laughter made him blink. Some performers had begun a little comical play, containing a generous amount of slapstick, mocking the Zlavic attempts at horse raiding, with the clever Kazakhs outwitting the dimmer southerners. Matteo joined in the laughter but knew the tomfoolery reflected more serious conflicts with deep roots in the Terrible Ages. He began reminiscing on how his passion for history had led him here.

The present day Kazakhs were the product of a confluence of ancient refugees from the war-shattered land of Kazakhstan, an epic diaspora from far away drought-parched Mongolia, and assorted displaced related ethnic groups who all merged to form the Great Zhuz. With their numbers as well as their spirits bolstered while populations around them were declining, the Kazakhs then steamrolled their way into the Ukrainian, southwestern Russia, and northeastern Romanian lands, either absorbing the inhabitants or driving them away on their own diasporas.

Teasing out the ancestries of the inhabitants of Eastern Europe and central Asia never ceased to fascinate Matteo. It led to his jumping at the opportunity to accompany a group of Deutslandic traders while on a visit to the Fifth Reich looking to access the history books they hoarded in their ancient libraries. The traders planned on journeying to the Kazakh homeland, in an effort to establish some commerce with the fierce easterners. Besides making a profit, the ultimate hopes were to promote friendly ties.

On discovering their goals, Matteo immediately dropped his plans to study at the Leibniz Archives of Hannover. Attempts to get permission to enter the libraries and do research had been an exercise in frustration comparable to pulling the teeth of a statue, especially since he lacked the gold that might have opened more than a few doors. Matteo's knowledge of the Kazakh language and culture plus the fact he was on sabbatical, ensured him a place on the caravan. The prospect of filling out the paucity of information about the history and current status of the peoples of these lands was irresistible. Perhaps he might get a hint of where that bolt of precious silk brought by a visiting Egyptian imam may have come from. In addition he looked forward to a bit of sightseeing.

He now looked back in embarrassment at how grossly he had underestimated the difficulty of the journey. The merchants employed well-armed guards for protection against robbers while they laboriously followed the ancient roads, all in poor shape from long neglect, leading into the Polish lands. Weaving their way through forested landscapes, they found scattered small farm holds and villages, some showing their Polish ancestry clearly while others were an odd mix of Old European and mid-Eastern cultures, descended from refugees displaced by the chaos of the Terrible Ages. They came across the vast crumbling ruins of old cities, some being mined for salvage by the locals, others played out and now all but invisible under the devouring vegetation. The guards, all Silesians, accompanied them as far as Krakow, then abruptly and without explanation abandoned them.

By now midwinter had set in, with howling winds and blowing heavy snows. Ice storms mingled with them, coating layers of thick glaze on buildings, trees, and the ground, which gleamed in the sun like crystal and made walking treacherous. The local people were hospitable enough but without guards it looked as if the trading expedition might fall apart and leave Matteo stranded with no means of getting back home. He recalled staring in misery out an old glass window at the ancient town blanketed in fresh snow, yearning for his home town of Milan, which now seemed so far away it might as well be on the moon.

But it seemed God was looking out for him. On a sunny late winter day, he ran into the mullah Tokbolat Smagulov, engaged in his own expedition visiting a small enclave of Kazakhs living in Krakow for as long as anyone could remember and practicing their religion: a syncretism of Old Islam, Christianity and elements of Judaism, similar to some of the other sects Matteo had encountered on his journey through the Polish lands. A tall, lean man with the Asiatic features typical of most Kazakhs, Tokbolat was searching for ancient manuscripts he hoped to add to a small but growing library he and the other mullahs had established. Striking up a conversation with the distressed bishop, he and Matteo quickly found common ground. Once Matteo explained his predicament to the mullah, Tokbolat generously invited him and the traders he had come with to join his own people when they journeyed back to their homeland.

Suddenly everything seemed brighter. The traders, delighted at the change in fortune, began a feverish preparation. Before long, Matteo, bundled in furs, and riding a strange two-humped camel (something he had seen in old drawings but originally thought a confused rendition of the dromedary camel), was headed east along with the mullah and his company. Kazakh warriors guarded the entourage and would occasionally prod their horses and charge high-spiritedly about, making mock attacks on each other. It was a disturbing reminder that these were the fearsome raiders who had made periodic incursions into Western Europe over the centuries.

But the Kazakhs showed unfailing good manners. Tokbolat had no hesitations answering Matteo's questions regarding their surroundings as well as the southern barbarians. The latters' animal rustling, metal and wood plundering were a source of perpetual aggravation to the Kazakhs, who the mullah insisted were a peaceful people unless attacked.

As they neared their destination, Matteo spotted a chilling sight. The well-travelled road ahead of them forked sharply, the left hand veering northward. The brush was slashed back a dozen meters from the road. Ancient concrete pillars framed the northern roadway on either side. Matteo judged them to be the remnants of some huge, long-vanished building. They towered high overhead, featureless except for the human skulls wedged into niches chiseled in the concrete. Small piles of skulls, both human and animal, also decorated the platforms the pillars sat upon. Tokbolat turned in his saddle, his face grim, and pointed. Wooden posts, the images of skulls carved into them, lined either side as far up the northern road as they could see.

"Chernobi," was all he said. The name, familiar to Matteo, sent a cold frisson of horror up the bishop's spine, causing him to make the sign of the cross. The traders, hearing the ancient name, also crossed themselves.

"This name is known to us," replied Matteo. "We have a few such places where I come from. They have many warning signs about as well, but sometimes it's hard to restrain the curious."

The mullah nodded soberly. "It is much the same here. You can tell all the tales of horror you wish or pile a thousand skulls as warning but there are always idiots who refuse to believe."

The caravan moved on in silence down the right hand road, the gruesome warning posts receding into the distance behind them. The Kazakh's lands were a pleasing mixture of pastureland, forest, and numerous grass-covered ruins, some with colorful flags over them marking the claim of a family clan to any metal or other valuable materials present. The winter snows had already begun dwindling away to widely scattered patches. Frothy white fair weather clouds sailed like clipper ships in the deep blue sky.

The contrast between the surrounding peaceful scenery and the frightful ruins of the ancient power plant north of them brought to mind the awesome power humans once possessed that caused the inadvertent creation of Chernobi and its counterparts around the world. In the past, Matteo often mused with regret over the lost knowledge and technologies of the ancients. But he had little doubt this was one science which better remained in the past, forgotten. Seeing the warning posts only reinforced his belief.

In a few days, they arrived at the city where the Khan's royal court was located. Rather than permanent stone or wooden buildings, the Khan and his family, their servants, mullahs, entertainers and assorted hangers-on were housed in a huge cluster of magnificently decorated yurts built around wooden frameworks which the mullah told him could be disassembled and moved at a moment's notice, should the need arise. The Kazakhs had never forgotten their nomadic customs in spite of the rise and fall of the powerful technical civilizations once occupying these regions. Matteo saw a certain poignancy in the sight of ancient ruins still visible here and there worked into the dwellings of the common folk living around the court itself.

The odor of cooking filled the air, mingled with the pungent smell of animal dung laid out to dry in the sun. It combined with the strong aroma of the beasts themselves, moving in great clusters about the city now that the weather was improving. Young boys and girls on ponies tended the herd animals: shaggy brown and white cattle, burly sheep heavy with winter wool, and above all, the famed horses carefully bred by the Kazakhs for strength and endurance.

"Oh, how wonderful!" blurted Matteo in delight as he watched the handsome creatures gallop effortlessly about, their manes and tails gleaming like spun gold in the sunlight. One magnificent palomino had a coat so shimmering he might well have been cast from the precious metal. No surprise, he wore a woven collar with the eagle emblem of the Khan.

"Thank you," grinned Tokbolat. "The raiders who come from the south seek these above all else."

"I can hardly blame them," replied Matteo. "If I wasn't such a slow runner, I might try to steal one myself!"

The mullah laughed. Out of the corner of his eye Matteo could see the yearning expression on the traders' faces. There was little doubt in his mind some of the stallions would, with prolonged haggling, wind up in herds far to the west.

It was while Tokbolat was pointing out the sights to Matteo that he caught his first glimpse of Ruslan Yussupov, moving at a brisk pace, followed close behind by his slave. The young man carried writing materials, his wooden slave collar around his neck. Matteo understood the collar could be easily removed if any slave was lucky enough to be manumitted. He was sure that did little to ease the servitude they were forced to endure until then. The slave following Ruslan kept his face carefully neutral, but Matteo saw a startled look of recognition and then sadness in the dark eyes as they fixed for a moment on the bishop's clothing. Doubtless he had been taken in a slave raid on the eastern Italian coast, as he had the look of a coastal Italian. Seeing Matteo's clerical garb must have brought back sorrowful memories for him.

Ruslan himself scattered the local residents with his long stride. It was obvious he expected no one to block his way and they obliged by moving quickly when they spotted his approach. Matteo saw many make a hurried gesture against the Evil Eye as they dodged him. He was startled to see the mullah quietly make a similar gesture, though a look of embarrassment came over Tokbolat's face when he realized Matteo had seen.

"It's hard not to," he confessed, his expression sheepish. He then explained who Ruslan was, telling Matteo of his abilities to forge metal and create gunpowder. "He carries an air of ill omen wherever he goes. If it wasn't for his secret of the exploding powder, I don't think the Khan would tolerate him, no matter what his other talents. I recommend you not cross him in any way. He holds grudges and would make a bad enemy."

Matteo suspected the warning was meant to circumvent any notions he might be harboring about rescuing the slave. As a stranger to this place, he knew any attempt on his part to free the young man would almost certainly backfire. Hard as it was, it was better to tolerate the situation. He was familiar enough with Kazakh custom to know slaves could win their freedom if they showed promise or did some great service for their masters. Ruslan's slave appeared well dressed and the writing materials in his possession suggested he was literate. In all likelihood he would liberate himself through his own efforts without any well-meaning bumbling by Matteo to free him.

The next few weeks found Matteo busy translating for the traders as they bartered with the Kazakh merchants. The locals expressed great interest in goods such as wines, cotton cloth, and glassware. As in many other places there was a tremendous hunger for any sort of metal. To his surprise, he found himself being often asked about the "smoking plant," which after a bit of confusion, he discovered to be tobacco. Evidently a few samples of the plant, a luxury import from the North American continent, had found their way to the land of the Kazakhs, piquing their interest, particularly in its medicinal properties.

When he wasn't interpreting, he spent time with Tokbolat, discussing history. Like Matteo, the mullah relished delving into the past, contemplating the ruins the ancients had left behind and the legacy they had, for better or worse, left the current inhabitants.

"I know from legend and the writings we have that mighty nations and people beyond numbering filled the world," said Tokbolat, as he carefully poured a small amount of tea into a cup for his guest. "Once when I was young, a great flood washed away a portion of land not far from here, exposing a huge pile of bones. They were just in a jumble, so I think it was a mass grave of some sort, not the usual cemetery that you find here and there. Nothing to tell how old it was. So many bones! I never saw anything like it before! There was no sign of violence on them, so it was thought some terrible epidemic or famine must have happened. But the idea of having so many people living at once is amazing to me. It's hard to visualize. Yet we see ruins everywhere showing there were once many people and the land wasn't really empty, the way the song-priests tell us."

"The ancients had an amazing knowledge of medicine, crop growing and animal breeding that allowed huge populations, but they paid a price for it," replied Matteo, sniffing appreciatively at his teacup. "I'm sorry to say they didn't show much wisdom when using the great power their sciences gave them. Chernobi is a good example. The radiant energy that makes it so dangerous also allowed them to build incredible machines. They seemed to believe it a worthwhile trade-off but they obviously never gave a thought to what they would be leaving their descendants."

"Our histories speak of these great wonders also," sighed the mullah. "But we know little or nothing of how they were made because the fanatics of previous centuries burned everything they could get their hands on, killing men and women of knowledge, claiming God was enraged over any kind of science and that was why He cursed the earth with terrible heat and storms. Praise be to God that madness finally faded away! When the Wandering Prophet came through two centuries ago, he enlightened us so at least we know better now why the world is the way it is. But if we are to rebuild the sciences, it must be done with wisdom for improving life, not just a way to vaunt ourselves."

"I once read an ancient text from another land that speaks of considering the effect for seven generations of any action we take," mused Matteo. "My own people long ago agreed that this was the best policy to have when deciding what knowledge to use from the past."

"Seven generations," repeated Tokbolat, smiling. "I like that. We trace back our family ancestries that way. I wonder what ancient wise one said that?"

"I don't know, but if more people had listened to him or her, Chernobi might not exist."

"I wish we could come up with better ways to bar people from exploring that place," said the mullah, his face glum, as he sipped at his own tea. "It's so hard to find workable metal here and there's always been rumors metal can be found there not poisonous to the touch. So far we've been fortunate only a few luckless ones have made the try and destroyed only themselves. We bury their bodies in lead boxes similar to that one." Tokbolat pointed at a small metallic box where he kept certain priceless books stored. "Along with anything they find. But I always worry that one day some poor fool will bring radiant material in amongst us and we'll discover it too late."

"Folly is difficult to discourage, I'm afraid." Matteo shook his head regretfully. "But if we can succeed in creating trade routes and begin commerce, metal that's safe to handle can be brought in from elsewhere. That may reduce the temptation."

"God willing," nodded Tokbolat. "Bekzat is certain to follow the lead of his father Arystanbek when he inherits the Khanate and keep the peace with your people in the west. But his brothers are sprouted from a different soil. They dream of the old days of raiding and plundering. They don't understand the richness they hunger for can be just as easily gotten through trade which doesn't carry the spiritual burden of murder, bloodshed and chaos. I and the other mullahs work hard to create schools and spread learning as the Wandering Prophet urged us to do. That can only happen if there is peace. God forbid the Terrible Ages return and plunge us back into darkness!"

Now in the Khan's yurt, as he watched jugglers spinning flaming torches and performing acrobatics while they did so, he found himself praying that the long-lasting peace he had known would continue. The traders he had accompanied were making successful connections with promises of future trade, which in time might make the Kazakhs powerful allies. But so much would depend on how well Bekzat could take over the rulership once his father passed away. As Matteo silently recited the ancient Peace Prayer of Saint Francesco, he had the odd feeling he was being watched. Shifting his gaze, he found Ruslan's slave staring at him. The young man had a beseeching expression on his face, and there was little mistaking the fear in his eyes. Before Matteo could draw Tokbolat's attention, the slave quickly averted his gaze, the expressionless mask that so many slaves wore reasserting itself.

When Matteo left the yurt with Tokbolat, he found that the mullah had also seen the look of fear.

"Could Ruslan be abusing him?" wondered Matteo. "It seems foolish that he would do so."

"It is," replied the mullah, clearly upset. "The laws protecting slaves from abuse are very stern. Of course, it doesn't stop the occasional beatings or rapes. Only ensures that slaves have some recourse if their masters mistreat them. I have never been at ease with slavery, especially after reading the old histories, telling how it had been outlawed in many lands. But the custom is deeply entrenched among us. Ruslan would never let go of a valuable slave, if he could help it, so it seems strange to think he might be causing harm to him. If there is abuse going on, I'm afraid it's up to—Cumar, I believe his name is—to approach me or one of the other mullahs for justice. Until then, we can do nothing."

Matteo sighed with resignation. Old habits and customs always resisted any effort to change or mitigate them. Tokbolat's status as a mullah, ironically, had the effect of restricting his actions, as he needed to uphold the laws and could not step outside them, even to help a slave in distress. Matteo wondered if there might be a way to encourage Cumar to make some move, perhaps visit Ruslan's forge under a guise of having something repaired. But he frowned and shook his head. It was tempting to devise plans but bitter experience had taught him long ago how easy it was to botch up, even with the best of intentions. Better to let God's guiding hand take care of such matters.

They retired to Tokbolat's yurt and talked well into the evening. The mullah showed great interest in the rediscovery of the Gutenberg printing press, which had been preserved by the various North American countries and brought back to the continent where it had been invented. Matteo described its delighted reception by his people and the chilly response of the Fifth Reich, which brought a gust of laughter from the mullah.

"So you think they were secretly hoarding the design?"

"Have you seen the books they produce? Because of that, most scholars suspect they did, myself among them. How else to explain their reaction?" chuckled Matteo. "You would think they'd welcome the return of the very device their own ancestors created. Instead they endlessly fulminated against the—how did they put it?—bizarre machines of the Americans, saying it would cause no end of chaos. Hmmph! The only thing it will cause is the loss of their monopoly on book production and knowledge preservation—"

"Hsst!" whispered Tokbolat, looking at the yurt flap. "Someone is there."

The mullah sprang to his feet and pulled aside the flap, revealing the terrified face of Cumar. The young man at once dropped to his knees and grasped Tokbolat's robe.

"Please . . . I dare not stay too long . . . he will suspect."

"What is happening, my son?" asked Matteo, coming over to stand beside the mullah.

"My master is plotting a terrible evil. He has been meeting with some men—I don't know who—they keep their faces hidden and he always makes me go into my quarters when they come." Cumar's dark skin had lost its underlying ruddiness and he trembled. "My master took one of the new slaves he bought and they went—oh God have mercy—they went to Chernobi!"

"What?" Tokbolat's face turned waxy with horror.

"My master came back alone. He wouldn't say what happened to the slave but he must have sent him into the Forbidden Place to get metal. He has it in a box just like that one." Cumar pointed at the lead box sitting near the guest table. "Then he used the other slave to test the poison of the metal inside so his visitors could watch its effect." Cumar wrung his hands in anguish. "Poor Muhamed died on his mat, his hair falling out. It took days! Terrible sores grew on his legs and he vomited until he choked on it. Ruslan buried him yesterday but I don't know where."

"Merciful Healer!" Matteo whispered, aghast. He crossed himself.

"Forgive me . . . I must go, before he realizes I am gone!" With that, Cumar leapt up and sprinted from sight, leaving Tokbolat and Matteo reeling in shock.

The two shaken men returned to their seats and stared at their cooling teacups.

"If we confront him, he will surely deny it," Tokbolat said at last. "He no doubt has the box well-hidden so a search would be useless. He would flee before the truth could be found out."

"And he would know Cumar approached us," grimaced Matteo, thinking of the unpleasant fate likely to fall on that brave young man at Ruslan's hands. Then his eyes fell on the lead box sitting in the yurt, its lid open, showing the ancient texts inside. The box was actually wood with thin lead sheets gilded onto it to protect against vermin. But it did look like the thick lead boxes radiant waste was buried in. He grew thoughtful as he looked at it. "But there might be a way . . ."

The next day was the final day of the New Day celebrations. The Khan's yurt was filled to brimming with feasting locals and visitors much like Matteo joining in the festivities. A group of young women performed a slow, elegant dance accompanied by the cheerful thrum of dombra and beating of drums. Matteo and Tokbolat sat in their usual positions, this time with the addition of a small wooden cart, its contents concealed by a heavy brocaded rug. They kept a close watch for the arrival of Ruslan.

"I have already alerted members of the Khan's guards I will be making an accusation," whispered Tokbolat into Matteo's ear.

"If only Ruslan will show," whispered back the bishop, his nerves quivering with anxiety.

"He always does. Don't forget, he likes making a late entrance to draw attention to himself." The mullah had a grim smile on his face. Matteo wished he had as much faith in the plan he had concocted as Tokbolat did. It had sounded good when the bishop first proposed it, but as the moment of truth approached, he could feel doubts surfacing. But there was no time for hesitation, for now Ruslan entered the royal yurt, striding as though he owned the place. Cumar shadowed him, his face holding its customary neutral look but his eyes betraying his despair. Matteo silently prayed as he and the mullah stood.

The music tapered off as the dancers withdrew. Brushing carelessly past them, Ruslan assumed his usual seat. Some in the crowd glared in resentment but they pushed away from him in their seats as if there was some foul miasma wafting about the dark clad figure. No one dared remonstrate with him. Well, that was about to change, thought Matteo, steeling himself. Both he and Tokbolat walked solemnly to the center of the yurt, Matteo pulling the little cart behind him. Seeing them, the crowd fell quiet, puzzled murmurs filling the air. Cumar watched wide-eyed, a wild hope lighting his gaze, as they neared both him and Ruslan. Tokbolat raised his arm.

"Mighty Khan, good guests, I stand before you with dire news." The mullah's face was stony, his right arm out straight holding his crozier. Matteo found himself admiring Tokbolat's flair for acting. "I have learned through the revealing hand of God that one amongst you has stolen treasure belonging to the Khan." He paused. "I accuse Ruslan Yussupov of conniving with members of your inner court to enrich himself at your expense!"

"That's a lie!" bellowed Ruslan, leaping to his feet, his face fiery red. The Khan sat erect, his eldest son beside him also sitting up. "I deny this accusation. I would never betray the Khan in such a fashion. I demand to know where this lie has come from!"

"No lie," replied Matteo, his voice loud and stern. "For here is the evidence!" With a flourish he pulled the rug off the box concealed under it, its dull grey metal gleaming in the sunlight coming through the open flaps of the Great Yurt of the Khan. "We found the treasure box he had hidden." Matteo, finding himself getting into the drama of the moment, tilted the box and dumped out a small pile of metal scraps and concrete.

Ruslan's reaction was immediate. He screamed in horror and threw himself on the ground.

"You fool! You fool! We'll all be killed!"

"We'll all be killed?" Matteo asked. His voice turned smug. "By mere scraps I collected from your own refuse pile which you leave out for the poor?" He set down the box Tokbolat had used to store books. Ruslan turned ashen. "No, Ruslan, I think not."

"Cumar," called Tokbolat. "As mullah of the royal court of the Great Khan, I place you under my protection and summon you to tell what you know."

The shaking young man rose and approached Tokbolat. Enraged and realizing he'd been tricked, Ruslan jumped back to his feet, reaching into his sash and pulling out a knife. However, the guards Tokbolat alerted had already moved into position and now rushed forward, seizing Ruslan before he could strike at Cumar. The smith could only watch with helpless fury while his slave repeated his story from the night before.

At the mention of Chernobi, an extraordinary silence fell over the crowd, so profound Matteo could hear the lowing of cattle in the distance. Cumar, his voice at first unsteady but then growing in confidence, spoke movingly of the awful death of Muhamed.

"Lies! All lies!" shrieked Ruslan.

"So where are the two slaves you purchased just last month?" replied Tokbolat, his expression cold. "When I questioned your neighbors this morning, they told me of how you had taken a wheelbarrow of hay and organic waste to the composting fields just after dusk a few days ago. They thought that was very odd of you. What was hidden in that wheelbarrow, hmm? Shall we look at the freshly dug areas? I don't believe it will be difficult to find the remains of the slave you so cruelly murdered."

"And what of the ones who conspired with you?" spoke the Khan ,Arystanbek, who had cast off his ornamental outer robes and approached Ruslan. "I think if my soldiers question you a bit, you will be happy to tell who they are."

"I do not think it is any great mystery," replied Bekzat, who had not left his position. "I suspect my brothers may know the answer to that, as they have been seen meeting with Ruslan before."

He turned to where his two younger siblings usually sat. Kirill was still on his bench, his face tense, but the spot beside him where Nurlan had been was empty. The young prince, evidently scenting where the wind was coming from, had fled in silence while everyone was distracted.

"Where is your brother?" asked the Khan, his voice deceptively mild. Kirill gaped in shock for a moment at the empty seat. Then, realizing the terrible position he was in, he stripped away his royal robes and, wearing only trousers, approached his father and threw himself prone at his feet.

"Father, I swear by the Lioness of the Earth and our Father in the Sky, that I knew nothing of the radiant poison. I knew only that Ruslan was promising us the Khanate if we would make him a member of the court. It was Nurlan who met the most with him. It was he who was plotting!"

Ruslan looked almost as grey as a corpse, not even bothering to protest. What could he say when a son of the Khan admitted in front of all gathered of the plot against his own father and Ruslan's involvement in it? Matteo could only shake his head at the folly of it all. The Khan himself straightened to a great height and glared down at Ruslan, his dark eyes glowing with fury.

"Long have I tolerated your presence, for the sake of the exploding powder, but no more! Have your ears been deaf to the song-priests? Did you not listen to how our ancestors were poisoned by their great enemies using the very radiant energy you toy with? Did it mean nothing to you to hear how our former lands were laid waste and how we were forced to flee to cleaner lands so that we might survive? We arose from those terrible ashes like the mighty phoenix and have become a great people again! But now you would make use of that ancient evil to win the status I know you crave!" The Khan's voice rose like thunder and Matteo saw the powerful man who lay buried within the aging flesh beginning to reemerge. "What did you intend to do? Poison me and Bekzat? Our physicians are not idiots! They would have realized what we were dying of and suspected the plot. You took advantage of my sons' greediness all for the sake of power. I, more than anyone here, can tell you how hollow that really is! Now you have lost all. There can be only one fate for you!"

"No! No! No!" screamed Ruslan. Wiry from years of blacksmithing, he broke away from the guards holding him, but only for a moment. Other guards rushed to intercept him. One, using the butt of his halberd, struck the frantic man across his knees and Matteo heard the horrid sound of bone breaking. Ruslan fell, moaning and cursing.

"What of the box of radiant waste?" asked Matteo, surprised by a stab of pity for the metalsmith.

"He has that hidden in the back of the forge," Cumar said. "I secretly watched to see where he was putting it. I can show you where."

"Then let justice be done," intoned the Khan. Without any fanfare, the guards dragged the wailing Ruslan out of the royal yurt so the place would not be soiled with blood. His keening faded into the distance and then with terrible abruptness cut off. A long somber silence filled the yurt. A guard emerged from a side entrance and coming over to the Khan, whispered into his ear. The ruler listened for a moment and nodded.

"Nurlan has fled with two of his retainers. He will be hunted down and subject to my judgement." He looked down at Kirill, who still lay prone at his father's feet, sweating and trembling. "You, I shall spare for now. You must tell all that you know of the plot against me and your brother. If you withhold nothing, then there is a chance you can redeem your honor. But if I catch you in one lie, your head will be seated on the entrance to the city along with Ruslan's."

The crisis seemed to have reinvigorated Arystanbek. As Bekzat came to stand beside him, the ruler of the Kazakhs smiled at Cumar.

"You have done well to reveal this plot." He raised his hand and placed it on Cumar's cheek. "It is my decree that from this moment forward, you are a freeman, able to go about where you will." He gestured and another mullah came forward, who took a small tool from his belt and clipped away two wooden stubs, allowing the slave collar to drop from Cumar's neck. Overwhelmed, the young man began weeping with joy as everyone in the yurt applauded. Both Tokbolat and Matteo, grinning broadly, applauded with them.

As the excitement died down and the festivities resumed, Tokbolat drew Cumar to one side.

"You are welcome to stay. Your writing skills would be very useful here."

"I thank you," replied Cumar, still dabbing at his eyes, "but I yearn to return to my homeland, the city of Forli, to see if my mother and sisters still live."

"I will be returning to the west at the beginning of summer. You can travel with me," said Matteo.

Cumar agreed to this arrangement and for the time being employed himself as a scribe for Matteo, which allowed him to revive his childhood language. Before he moved into the guest dwelling with the bishop, he returned to the forge to retrieve his few belongings. Matteo was astonished to see the young man reemerge not only with a small pouch of writing implements but also an enormous bundle wrapped tight in animal skins. There were guards of the Khan waiting beside the yurt and they stepped aside, their expressions curious, as Cumar carried the awkward armload past them. Once he was done, they went inside with torches to burn the yurt.

The lead box with radiant waste had already been buried in a distant place along with the body of the unfortunate Muhamed, who was discovered after only a short search. All salvageable metal was stripped from the forge as it was too valuable to waste. Ruslan's remaining possessions were burnt to ashes and holy water sprinkled on the site. There were many who believed he had been in league with dark forces and they celebrated while the yurt went up in flames.

That evening, as Matteo served tea to Tokbolat who had stopped by for a visit, the bishop could no longer contain his curiosity and asked Cumar what was in the bundle.

"I am surprised Ruslan allowed so many possessions for you. Is this paper? Ingredients for ink?"

"No," replied Cumar, a bit shamefaced. "This actually belonged to Ruslan but I couldn't bear the thought of them burning it."

"What is it?" asked the mullah, intrigued.

"Some books. Well, four books, really. They are in a strange script I cannot read. But Ruslan could. He said they belonged to his mother as part of her dowry and she taught him how to read them."

As Cumar spoke, he pulled out the bundle and slowly began untying it. Matteo's ears pricked up at the mention of it being part of a dowry. It was not unusual for old preserved books to be included as part of marriage portions, or as a method of payment for various economic transactions. The older, the better. He and Tokbolat watched as the former slave with much care pulled back each animal skin covering the bundle. As he reached the final one and removed it, Matteo quickly drew in his breath.

Four large, extremely thick books were revealed. Inspecting their worn dark covers, he could see they were very old indeed. Tingling with excitement, he leaned forward.

"May I touch?"

"Yes, of course. They are not mine anyway but Ruslan valued them so much. Their condition is very delicate so please take care."

"Oh, I would do no less."

Tokbolat watched fascinated as Matteo, using infinite care, gently supported the cover of the top book as he gingerly opened it so its weight would not cause the binding to tear. His finger almost trembled as he examined the title page just inside the cover.

"It's Cyrillic, that's why you couldn't read it," whispered Matteo, who told Cumar the Cyrillic script had long ago been rejected during the Terrible Ages by many who retained their literacy but did not want to use the writing of their former conquerors. "In the west we use the ancient Latin alphabet as we always have, but other places such as here use the Arabic scripts instead. I know of only a few groups far to the north who still write in Cyrillic."

"I can read a bit of Cyrillic, if it's in a language I know," confessed Tokbolat.

"What odd looking writing. I wonder why they made it so large? What does it say?"

"This is not hand script. It is machine printing." Replied Matteo, no longer able to contain his excitement. "Made large for those who had poor vision. I've seen books like this before."

"Machine printing?" said Cumar, puzzled. "You mean like the printing press you told me about?"

"Yes, but I think an automatic machine made this. Possibly one of the last. These books, in my estimation, date from the end of the twenty-second century. There's no printing date so it's hard to be sure."

"We have a few machine printed books," said Tokbolat, becoming excited himself. "During the early Terrible Ages, the ancestors began using durable paper they hoped would last a long time, made of hemp, animal skins and other natural substances. Nothing like plastic that might deteriorate or wood pulp that would crumble. But come now Matteo, you're holding out on us! What is the title of the book? It looks like the Ruskai language but I cannot read that."

"The Complete Writings of Leo Tolstoy," read Matteo with great reverence.

"Tolstoy? Who could that—no wait, I know the name," said the mullah. "He was an ancient Ruskai, who lived over a thousand years ago."

"Yes, he was a nobleman but possessed of deep spirituality. He loathed war and its destruction. He even wrote a book called *War and Peace*. There are preserved copies of that and a few other of his writings but many of his works were lost during the Terrible Ages."

"And this says the complete writings!" cried Cumar, finally understanding the bishop's elation.

"Yes, Ruslan's ancestors must have somehow come into possession of these books and, because it was the writings of one of their great ones, preserved them through the generations. Incredible! It's a miracle of God that they managed to escape destruction."

"Yes," said Tokbolat. "The Burners of Blasphemy would not have spared such books. They hated anything of the Ruskai almost as much as they hated science."

"Ruslan said his mother was a Ruskai," said Cumar. "She was a secondary wife, not of high status. But he revered her and the books he inherited from her. The only time I ever saw gentleness in his face was when he read from this book."

"All human beings are a mixture of good and evil. Ruslan was no different. We can be grateful he took care to preserve the books and of course his respect for them is what prompted you to save them. I'm sure the guards would not have bothered looking for such a treasure as this." Matteo gently ran his fingers over the paper, regret shadowing his face. "The books are too fragile for me to risk bringing them back to the west for translation and copying. It will be better to keep them here."

"Well, if you send us one of those printing presses, we can copy them ourselves and spread them about so they will not be lost again," said Tokbolat, beaming with delight. "I know of six scholars gifted in knowledge of Cyrillic and the Ruskai language. It would be a good way for them to educate their own students and expose them to some of the old wisdom writings as well."

"I can certainly do so, as long as you promise to send me the first copy you make!" laughed Matteo. The bishop turned back to the ancient books and carefully turned pages until he stopped and lingered over one paragraph that caught his eye. As Tokbolat and Cumar listened, their eyes shining in the firelight, he began to read aloud.

"*Love is life. All, everything that I understand, I understand only because I love . . . Love is God, and to die means that I, a particle of love, shall return to the general and eternal source.*"

The Road to Finx: Pedro's Tale

by Rita Rippetoe

‡‡‡‡"Terrible Tidings. Warnings. Sanctuaries of Sin." Bold words printed in large letters. "Tonite at the Meeting House. Come and be Warned by Brother Matt Long and Sister Megan Maple. Talk begins at Sundown. No children under the age of 12." Stamped in red ink at the bottom of the poster: "Approved by the Sweetwater Meeting Elders."

"See, it's approved," exclaimed Pedro, pointing at the small print. "Papa will have to let us go."

"If your chores are done," replied the gray-haired woman beside him. It was unlike her fifteen year old nephew to be so interested in an event at the Meeting House, but she supposed that a chance to hear anyone from outside was difficult to resist. The radio provided some novelty in the two hour evening broadcast, but news bulletins and speeches by The Supervisor didn't interest the young people much.

Sweetwater was short on entertainment for young or old. Like many towns in the American Southwest it had started as a stage stop, developed into a small town serving local ranchers, and then blossomed into a resort and retirement community. Retirement—now there was an idea whose time had passed. Most people these days only retired into a grave, unless they crippled up or turned senile to become a burden on their families for a few years first. With that bitter thought, Aunt Alice picked up her shopping basket and shooed Pedro down the cracked sidewalk to her next stop.

Alejandro's Pharmacy also had a flyer in the window. Aunt Alice pointed at it when she reached the counter. "Know anything about that?"

"Just what the flyer says, Ms. Wilson." Jason Alejandro wasn't a member of the Meeting House, but it was impolitic to refuse to display their announcements. The pharmacist was a respected professional in town, but Catholics were viewed as little better than heathens by some Meeting folks. "We don't get the Warners, but Father Michael has told us about the Sanctuaries. That used to mean something sacred, but now they are places where all kinds of sin prospers."

"What kinds of sin? Robbing and killing?" Pedro asked.

Alejandro glanced at Ms. Wilson before replying. "That's the sort of thing you need to ask your father or your aunt, or wait to hear it from your Meeting Elders. Not for me to be saying." He turned back to Ms. Wilson, "What can I help you with today?"

"I have a sample jar of the peach preserves I just put up. Let me know what kind of trade we can make for my brother's medications." She pulled a pint mason jar from her basket, its wax seal covered with a square of faded calico, and set it on the counter.

"I'll be happy to. I'll send a message when I work it out. When is Mr. Smithers going to have another batch of that peach brandy ready? I can really sell that."

"Well the last lot has aged a year. But he's thinking of sending some on the next Peddler's Train that passes through. We'll keep back a couple of kegs for you though. And some of the raw potato spirits for your medicines," she said. "You have a blessed day, now."

"Bless you and yours also, Ms. Wilson."

That evening Pedro and his father Andrew Smithers dressed in their go-to-meeting clothes. Clean shirts with collars buttoned on and bolo ties. Grey woolen pants and suspenders. It being May, they wore vests instead of jackets, embroidered with the Christian fish symbol, the intertwined triangles of the trinity and the chi-rho that everyone called the crossed P.

"Are you sure you don't want to come, Aunt Alice?"

"No," she said, "I'd rather finish up this shirt. And I think that mare might be a bit early to foal. Don't want just Buster here to handle that."

The meeting house was crowded and the shutters along each side were open for ventilation. Pedro and Andrew took their regular place in the family pew, but welcomed a couple of non-Meeting people to join them as the room filled up. They all stood as the Reverend walked to the center of the choir platform.

"Although this is not a regular Meeting, I will ask a blessing before introducing our guests." Heads bowed and hands clasped as he began. "Almighty God, grant that the knowledge we gain this night will guide us to actions holy in Thy sight. Amen."

A middling-sized black man with grizzled hair clipped short stepped forward alongside a tall blonde woman with a pale, freckled complexion. The man was dressed in a black suit, unbleached cotton shirt and a town-style tie hanging over his shirt front. His companion wore her hair in two braids wound into buns on either side of her head. She was clad in a blue cotton shirtwaist dress that reached to mid calf. Both wore traveler's sandals over bare feet: leather straps and rawhide soles painted with natural tar for traction and longer wear.

The pair smiled and nodded as the reverend introduced them, "Brother Matthew Long, Sister Megan Maple. These fine folks are members of the Warners."

"Sanctuary," the black man said, letting the word hang in the air for a moment. "That used to mean something holy. It's in the Bible, God's Holy Book. The Israelites are told to set up sanctuary cities for those accused of murder, to prevent blood vengeance from destroying society.

"But now this word has been corrupted. So called Sanctuary Cities are cesspools of sin. Corrupt officials set aside an area that is outside the Regulations. Oh, they'll send in their armed men to drag out a killer or a thief, a usurer or a rapist. Their citizens wouldn't stand for that sort to be sheltered and allowed to come and go preying on the city. But these officials accept payment to give sanctuary to worse criminals than those that merely kill your body or steal your earthly goods. They give shelter to people who sell drugs that warp your mind; drugs that make you question God and His ministers. They give shelter to heretics. People who question the Teachings and the Regulations. Worshippers of false gods. People who teach lies about the real God. People who deny Jesus. People who have been driven out of good towns like Sweetwater."

Pedro started to grow restless. This wasn't as interesting as he had hoped. Still, it was a change from weaving willow baskets while his father read from the Bible or the Teachings of Elder Buckley. Pedro came alert when the lady began to talk.

"I am pleased to see young people here to learn about the hazards that lurk in the world outside of your township. The material that Brother Matt and I are about to discuss is of a delicate nature. Because of this, I am asking that the men present rise and follow Brother Matt out to the ramada. As they move out the women will please move forward so as to hear me clearly."

Pedro duly followed his father out. The ramada tables had all been moved to the rear and the benches arranged in rows at the end furthest from the main meeting house. Looking back, Pedro saw that the deacons had closed the meeting house shutters on the side facing the ramada. What were they going to talk about that wasn't fit for women to hear?

Brother Matt walked between the rows of benches. "I don't want to have to shout out the vile information that it is my duty to give you tonight. I was talking inside of sins. Terrible sins. Terrible dangers to your souls. But there is worse to tell. You good men all read your Bible. You know that the Lord has forbidden certain sins of the flesh.

"Now, there are ordinary sins of the flesh. Humans are weak. We have an animal nature that is difficult to deny. Gluttony is a sin, but it is a sin that announces itself. You can't miss a fat man with his belly hanging down. Greed is a sin, but in a small community everyone knows who tries for more than their share. It is easy to shun the man or woman who sports fine garments or hoards the necessities of life while others go bare or hungry. Sloth is a sin, but the slothful man will not prosper in these hard times. Few are willing to labor so that another may take his ease. Wrath is a sin, one of the worst, but our meeting elders and our officers of law deal with those whose ungoverned wrath leads to assault or even murder.

"Lust is a sin. And just as we must have appetite, which ungoverned becomes gluttony, lest we die of hunger and thirst, so must we have a measure of sexual appetite, which ungoverned becomes sinful lust, lest the race die out for lack of offspring. I'm not here to talk about the natural lusts that sometimes lead men to acts they ought not to do. Fornication is a sin but it can be repented and mended by marriage. Adultery is a sin, but it can be mended by repentance and sometimes by voiding marriages. And after a year of prayer and repentance both parties may find new partners better suited. Jerking your peck is a sin." The man paused while a ripple of edgy laughter swept through the younger men and boys. "But, jerking your peck may be better than drawing another into sin through fornication. It may be better than adultery. It may be better than bothering your spouse when she is ill or out of sorts or tired to death from nursing an infant." This time the older men nodded understanding.

Pedro started to grow restless again. Everyone knew about sin. All the sins this Warner had mentioned had been the subject of more than one sermon by the Reverend.

"But there are unnatural lusts. Acts that are whispered about. Acts that are that joked about, with a nervous laugh and a look over the shoulder. Acts that thinking about makes a normal man gag. I see you older men nodding. These things aren't new. These things were already old when God gave the Israelites their laws. These things were old when St. Peter wrote to the new Christian churches about them.

"Some people don't think they should be spoken of. But does not speaking about rattlesnakes keep them from biting? No. And so long as the Good Lord sees fit to let rattlesnakes roam the land we praise them for devouring vermin, but we would be fools not to teach our children how to recognize them and how to avoid them."

Good grief, Pedro thought. When was the man going to get to the point? He glanced at his father, who looked puzzled.

"Unnatural lusts. Men who kiss other men lustfully. Men who touch another man's privates, or let theirs be touched. Men who use their privates in ways that the Lord did not intend." The men on the crowded benches shifted uneasily and looked around anxiously at the teens among them. "Yes, brothers. I am going to say these things. These things happen. And if a young man hasn't been warned explicitly, how can he protect himself? How can he say boldly, and with certainty, 'Stop, this is a sin!' You young men: if you haven't been told about men who would want to put their mouth on your peck what are you going to say when you meet one? Men who would want to put their peck in your mouth. Men who want to put their peck in your dark hole or want you to put your peck in theirs. You need to know that such men exist and that you should shun them and their ways." Matt paused and looked around. "Anybody bring a flask?"

One of the men in front stood up and handed him a leather flask. "Good potato spirits, Mr. Long."

Long took a mouthful of liquor, swished it around his mouth and turned to spit it out in the dry dust.

"That's better. Just the words leave my mouth foul. But now you got no doubt what I'm talking about. These Sanctuaries shelter people who live like that. Men who do such things with one another. Men who violate nature by dressing as women. Men who live together as though they were married. They can live there and work without fear of the Regulations.

"Now, I gotta talk dirty again. Ms. Maple is telling the same to the sisters. There are women who commit these sins also. Dress like men. Live with other women. Rub their naked woman parts together. Put their mouths down there. Use fake pecks to satisfy each other.

"And there are women who seem normal. They have normal sex with men, but they do things to keep from having children. They reject God's gift of fertility. They allow a garden to be planted, but they hoe it up before it fruits." He took another dramatic swig of liquor and spat again. "I repeat. These people live in the Sanctuaries without fear of the Regulations.

"You citizens know the penalties. But, thank God, these cases don't come up very often, so you may never have heard of a trial for sodomy; that's the legal term for the things I described. The penalties are heavy. First conviction, one year in the work crew. Second conviction, life in the work crew. Of course you all know that 'life' in the work crew is not as long a sentence as a stranger might think. It's just a death sentence that gets some use out of a criminal before hard work on harder rations sends him to the final Judgment."

Pedro leaned forward, his mouth hanging open. People actually did the things he had been confused by dreaming about? Kissing another man? Letting a man you liked touch your peck? Other things he hadn't even thought of. He only knew that when he went swimming with the other boys he had to stop himself from looking at their half-naked bodies. That he wanted to touch them, stroke their chests, run his hand down their backs and cup their butts in his hand. He knew that thinking about such things made his peck hard. He glanced around and saw that other young men seemed equally amazed by the things they were hearing. Did any of them have the same feelings? How would a person ever find out? No one wanted to go on the work crew. Three years ago a man in town had been sentenced to six months for stealing a sheep. He was almost a skeleton when he returned.

"Now you're all wanting to know where these terrible places are. Are you likely to blunder into one of these dens of sin by accident? Sister Megan and I travel the Colorado Territory of the Texas Public. Our remit goes over to Lost Angels, up to Denner and Sallac, down to the Mescan border. It probably won't surprise you at all to know that there is a Sanctuary City near Lost Angels. It's called Samona and it is over on the coast. Auro, outside of Denner, is another. Sallac had one twenty years back. But the Great Mormon Uprising put an end to that. The Mormons may be heretics, but they know how to drive sin from among their people. Finx, over to Zona has one too. Now, I know you folks in Sweetwater mostly trade with All-bekirk. But some things have to come from Finx and some of you go to Finx to sell your wares.

"The main thing you need to know about Sanctuaries is that they are in a separate quarter of town. You can go to Auro or Finx without ever setting foot in one. They are fenced and patrolled. Anyone who comes to the gate has to acknowledge that they are setting foot outside of the Regulations and cannot complain in court if they see a violation. Anyone who, God forbid, wants to stay, must appeal to the Jeffe and the Madam. Anyone who dwells in a Sanctuary has to wear a badge if they go outside, and be back in the gates before dark. They aren't allowed to marry or live outside the Sanctuary unless they repent in front of the Elders and go to a Cleansing.

"So, on one hand Sister Megan and I have come to warn you about the existence of these places of depravity. But on the other hand we have come to reassure you that you can go about your business; buy, sell, and travel without fear. You can go to the evil, God forbid, but the evil cannot venture out to claim you." He paused, then said, "Thank you for your attention. Bless your days and your homes."

The Reverend stood up. "Bless your steps, Warner Matthew. If you follow me, my wife has dinner ready at the house."

"You seem awful quiet," Alice said as she passed the squash to Pedro. "Was the Warning what you expected?"

Pedro shook his head. "Mr. Long told about some dirty things. He washed his own mouth out with spirits two times. Talked about things I never heard of before."

"Well, Mr. Long was correct saying some people don't believe in talking about those things," said Andrew. "Particularly at the dinner table. If you have questions you can ask me or one of the Elders later." Andrew speared the last pork chop and accepted the bowl of squash.

Pedro bent to his own plate, stirring butter into the squash. He knew he could never talk to his father about such things.

The next day at school the teens who had attended the Warners Meeting were surrounded by curious classmates. They broke into small groups of intimates to discuss what they had heard.

"My grandfather told me that those things the Warners talked about were legal back before the Red Revolt." This from Pedro's friend Benjamin, who swept out the pharmacy and made deliveries after school was out.

"Mom has a cousin lives up in Fornia," said Owen, whose mother taught the primary grades. "Mom reads her letters out to us. She said there were some people up there trying to get laws like our Regulations. But they were beaten in the last election. Seems most of the Elgeebeeta people took in orphans to raise after the government stopped having money to do it. Made a lot of people grateful to them. Especially after the Nigerian flu killed almost half the grown people in some parts. Cousin Brenda wrote that letting people live their own way as long as they don't rob or kill is part of Fornia values."

"What the heck is an Elgeebeeta?" asked one of the boys on the fringe of the group.

"It's shorthand for all the words that mean men liking men and women liking women and people that don't want to be the sex that God made them. Mom says there was lots of them in the old times and a lot of them went to Fornia from other places during the Revolt 'cause people on the Red side was rounding them up to kill them. She says a lot live up in the Northwest Territories and over east in New Atlantic too."

"Sounds to me like Fornians are next to heathens," Benjamin said. "How can you have a decent country without the Regulations?" The school bell put an end to the discussion.

A week later most of the discussion of the Warners had died down. Even the densest rowdies had tired of joking about unnatural sex, and the more intelligent had little time to wonder about the strange drugs that could make you question God or to speculate about the types of heresy sheltered in the distant cities.

The new topic of conversation was the Peddlers Train. An outrider had arrived on Saturday and the farmers and merchants in town were busy making lists of needed supplies and packing up merchandise for sale in the distant markets.

‡‡

"You're going to Finx, too. That's great. I didn't think I would know anyone on the trip." Pedro clapped Benjamin on the shoulder. "Dad is sending me along with the kegs of brandy. Aunt Alice was against it. Said I was too young. But Dad said fifteen is a good age to have an adventure, see some of the territory, before I settle down and think about family. And he says I'm big enough no one should give me much trouble." Pedro didn't dare add, even to his best friend, that he intended to check out the Sanctuary in Finx. The Warner's talk had raised questions he didn't dare ask anyone around him. Now that clear pictures of tantalizing but forbidden activities had replaced his vague desires to touch and be touched by the boys he had crushes on, he couldn't live his whole life out in Sweetwater without learning what kind of man he was.

"Mr. Alejandro is paying for me to go to the university," Benjamin replied. "They teach a two year course in pharmacy. He says he's been hoping for a clerk smart enough to be worth the cost. Had one ten years ago, but he died of the Nigerian flu before he could go. I just hope I can pass the entrance tests. I don't want to disappoint him."

"Well, it's good to have someone my age to ride with, even if you won't be coming back soon."

The Peddlers Train was forming up in the stockade outside the town gates. Benjamin Cassidy had letters of credit from Mr. Alejandro in a rubber lined pouch in his inner vest pocket. His mother had packed for him: shirts, socks, work pants, city pants and jacket for school, a warm coat, undershirts, handkerchiefs, extra boots and his one pair of city shoes. Tooth brush and tooth powder, and a couple of cakes of homemade soap completed his necessities. To these Benjamin had added Mr. Alejandro's extra copy of the pharmaceutical formulary, the thick notebook in which he had recorded everything he had been taught so far, a sealed bottle of ink, a pen, some pencils and an empty notebook. He was as ready as could be for the courses that Mr. Alejandro was paying for. He had about twenty dollars of his own in cash, although the coins were a combination of various old time Fed coins, Texas Repub coins and even the odd centavo piece. After some thought he had put half the money deep inside his packed goods and the other half in a bag secured to his belt. He turned to his mother for his goodbyes.

"I don't have to tell you to work hard. I just wish your father had lived to see you going off to the university. Bless Mr. Alejandro for his generosity." She hugged him fiercely. "I'll miss you so much. But knowing you'll have a profession that will keep you and a family and be valuable to your fellow man is worth it." She looked up at the sound of the Train leader's bell, gave Benjamin one last kiss and stepped back into the crowd.

On the other side of the train Pedro went through a similar scene with his father, solemnly shaking his hand before his aunt led the three of them in a prayer for his well being and safe return. She ended with a kiss on his cheek and a quick gesture to flick tears from the corners of her eyes. Pedro had already repeated to his father the list of instructions about the dozen kegs of peach brandy he was accompanying west. He knew the price he should get, how to secure the money in a letter of credit, and what supplies he should purchase to bring back home. Now that it was time to move out he swung astride the riding mule his father had rented from the Train and reined it into line.

The Train traveled slowly. On rough or hilly stretches the men and mules could make ten miles a day at most. On the long stretches of former Highway 60 they could average fifteen. But each stop at a town to trade meant at least a day of downtime. A few towns were off the main road and added more miles. It was a pretty average trip. A small group of bandits attacked just past the old state line, but the riflemen of the Train fought them off in short time. One passenger broke a collarbone when his horse reared and threw him during the shooting. And one mule ran off the road and managed to shed its load before being hunted down. It was a provision mule, so Mr. Miller, the Train Master, had to buy replacement supplies at the next stop. Another delay when a summer storm flooded one of the innumerable gullies they had to cross. Old timers sat around the fires at night and told tales of storm, flood, bandits, wild animal attacks, bad water and other perils they had endured on earlier trips.

Pedro had a little surprise a couple of weeks into the trip when he discovered that the new mule-driver who had hired on in Sweetwater was actually a schoolmate of his from back home, Chastity Gutierrez, who was passing as a boy named Chas. She begged Pedro not to give her away when he recognized her. She had run away from home rather than marry a well-off neighbor who had been courting her. Having seen her sister-in-law die in childbirth, she told Pedro that the thought of going to bed with a man just made her blood run cold. He agreed to keep the secret. It was probably too late for the Train Master to send her back anyhow.

The road they were following turned from northwest to due west. Letters formed by white-washed rocks against a hillside announced "Apache Junction." The road was coming off a hillside and those with sharp eyes or binoculars could see tall buildings in the distance.

"We must be close to Finx if we can see the buildings from here," Pedro remarked to the man riding beside him.

"Naw, we're still thirty some miles out. We can see those buildings because they're taller than anything you've seen before. Some are fifty or sixty stories. Course hardly anyone goes up in them. Half a day to climb the stairs and nothing up there when you do." The man who spoke was at least seventy years old with sparse white hair sticking out from under a leather hat brim. Despite his age he was ramrod straight, sitting his buckskin pony like the ex-cavalry man he was.

"Why'd they build them so tall if they were not used?"

"Back in the Oil days there was electric to run elevators. Didn't have to climb the stairs. You just walked into a box that was pulled up and down by a big wire cable. Some of them went so fast it made your stomach lurch, like when you swing on a long rope out over the swimming hole."

Pedro would have thought the old man was pulling his leg if he hadn't been able to see the buildings. Who would lie about something they would be proved wrong on in only a few days? *A few days.* That was all the time he had to make decisions that could change his life forever.

The next two days of travel were strange. For the past month they had been riding through mostly open country punctuated by towns like Sweetwater and its surrounding ranches. Now the road was lined by ruins, fragments of wall sticking up from crumbling concrete foundations of what had been individual homes. Sometimes a line of brush or small trees indicated the bed of a small creek or canal. Occasional clusters of larger buildings stood up, former shopping districts with empty window frames, faded signs and parking lots taken up by weeds.

Eventually they began to see signs that roads were being maintained. Potholes were filled in and a work crew was cutting the brush that grew in the pavement cracks. An actual highway sign gave the distance: "Phoenix 17 miles."

"What's that say?" Benjamin asked Mr. Miller.

"That's the way they spelled Finx back when this was the capital of the state of Arizona. It was named after a mythical bird that made a nest, laid an egg and set the nest on fire and died in the fire as the egg hatched. It was a story from the old days and the old country across the Atlantic ocean."

"You know an awful lot of history for a Train Master."

"Wasn't always a Train Master. Used to teach English at the University of the Second Texas Republic in Austin. Got bombed out by the Fed forces during the third attempt to retake the territory, joined up with the Public Guard. After the war I drifted around and eventually started wrangling for a train up to Danner and back. Worked my way up and here I am, Master of my own Train. I go from Finx to Allbekirk and back. Sometimes for variety I take a Train to Lost Angels, or up north to Danners."

Miller rode back through the train as they made their way down the last stretch of road, now shared with bicycles, horse drawn wagons and carriages and even, once, a bio-diesel powered Guard patrol cycle.

The next morning, Mr. Miller gave the wranglers instructions about how and where to unload their mules and where to pick up their pay. Merchants were reminded where to go to check their merchandise and how to file any claim for missing or damaged items. Some asked about transferring to a Train headed on to Lost Angels or down to the Border.

Pedro and Benjamin rode together. "Doggone it, Pedro, if this isn't the biggest bunch of people ever piled together How long do you have before you have to join up for the trip back? I wouldn't mind some company from home to explore a little."

"I've got til the fourteenth, Monday after this," Pedro said.

"Maybe we could invite Chas, too," Benjamin said. Then he added, "You do know that Chas is really Chastity run off from home?"

"You recognized her too?" Pedro said. "Sure. I suppose since people think she's a boy, no one will remark if we explore together." Pedro looked around to see if any of the older men were listening before continuing. "Listen, remember the Warners? Danged if I wouldn't like to just look inside that Sanctuary place, just to see." He glanced at Benjamin to gauge his reaction.

"Well, as long as we didn't get into any trouble. I don't dare disappoint Mr. Alejandro after all he's done for me. The first thing I have to do is find the university and sign up to take the tests. I should get that done the first day here."

"I've got to get this brandy sold and buy the supplies Dad ordered. So I'll be busy too. How about we plan to head over there our second afternoon if our work is done. And I wouldn't be surprised if Chas wants to go, too."

Two days later, Pedro, Benjamin, and Chas stood in the shadow of a building across from the Sanctuary gates. The Sanctuary walls were about twenty feet high, with guard towers on the corners. The gates stood open and men and women passed freely in and out one side. Pedro noted that those people all wore a palm sized patch of bright green on their left shoulder. That must be the badge that identified them as dwellers in the Sanctuary. On the other side of the gate visitors were being quizzed, patted down for weapons and made to read a large sign posted on the gatehouse before entering.

"Well, here goes nothing," declared Chas, and walked across the twenty feet of pavement to the gate. She didn't look back, but knew that Benjamin and Pedro were right behind, trying not to be obvious greenhorns.

"Business?" the guard asked as Pedro and Benjamin approached.

"Visiting," Pedro muttered. He had been surprised to hear Chas firmly proclaim "Sanctuary" in answer to the question.

The guard nodded and passed him on to a pair of guards behind him. "Who do you want to search you?"

"What difference does it make?"

"Women usually prefer to be searched by a woman, men by a man. Your choice."

The two young men were patted down by male guards, Chas by a young woman in uniform.

"Read the notice."

VISITORS MAY NOT CARRY WEAPONS: KNIVES, SWORDS, GUNS, BOWS, CROSSBOWS, EXPLOSIVES, CLUBS OR ANY OTHER OBJECT OR SUBSTANCE JUDGED DANGEROUS BY GATE CONTROL.

PERSONS OF ALL RACES, RELIGIONS, LANGUAGES AND CUSTOMS ARE WELCOME IN SANCTUARY.

PERSONS OF ALL GENDER EXPRESSIONS ARE WELCOME IN SANCTUARY.

REGULATIONS AGAINST THEFT, PERSONAL ASSAULT, MURDER, KIDNAPPING, SEXUAL ASSAULT AND FRAUD ARE IN FULL EFFECT IN SANCTUARY. VIOLATORS WILL BE HANDED OVER TO THE CITY GUARD. BEING OFFENDED BY THE IDENTITY, CUSTOMS, IDEAS OR GENDER EXPRESSION OF A VISITOR OR RESIDENT WILL NOT BE CONSIDERED EXTENUATING CIRCUMSTANCES.

REGULATIONS AGAINST CONSENSUAL SEXUAL RELATIONS, EXPRESSION OF NON-CONFORMING GENDER IDENTITY, AND REPRODUCTIVE FREEDOM ARE NOT IN EFFECT IN SANCTUARY.

REGULATIONS AGAINST THE USE OF FORBIDDEN DRUGS ARE NOT IN EFFECT IN SANCTUARY. LEAVING SANCTUARY WITH SUCH PRODUCTS IS AT YOUR OWN RISK.

REGULATIONS AGAINST TEACHING OR DISCUSSION OF ANY TOPIC, INCLUDING RELIGIOUS HERESY, POLITICAL IDEAS AND FORBIDDEN INFORMATION ARE NOT IN EFFECT IN SANCTUARY. LEAVING SANCTUARY WITH PRINTED MATTER IS AT YOUR OWN RISK.

"What the heck is gender expression?" queried Benjamin.

"I think it's women dressing as men or men as women. Like the Warners talked about. It's against Regulations, except for fun, like a costume party. Penalty is being whipped and put in the Reformatory for six months."

"The rest is the sex stuff they talked about. The way I read it, if a man asks you to put his peck in your mouth or any of those other things, you can't get mad and hurt him, like you might back home, unless he tries to force you," commented Pedro.

"That's correct, young man. Now are you and your friends ready to sign?"

"Sure thing." They each scrawled a signature on the sheet. Chas was led off to one side, waving a quick goodbye to her companions.

"Let's meet back here at dawn," said Benjamin. "I think we might want to explore on our own so's not to be embarrassed." Pedro nodded and strode off.

Pedro walked quickly into the busiest street he could see. He didn't know exactly what he was looking for, but was sure he didn't want anyone from home to be with him when he found it. A few blocks in he noticed a building with a brightly painted sign proclaiming, "See Sin—You Know You Want To—50¢." Men, and a few women, were going in and out, paying a cashier who stood at the door. Pedro checked the area for any familiar faces and sidled up to the man, holding out his half dollar.

"What exactly am I paying for?" He looked through the door at rows of little curtained booths. They reminded him of the ones put up every election year for the voting.

"First time here? Well, each booth has pictures of people naked or having sex. Some are slideshows. Some are still photos or drawings. Some are moving pictures. Pay your admission and you can spend as much time as you want. Just don't hold one booth too long. If an usher knocks, finish and move on. And use the towels provided; no one else wants to touch your peck juice."

Pedro blushed when he realized that the man assumed he would be jerking his peck in the booths. Well, he was here to see the sin, wasn't he? This seemed like a pretty safe way to get a sample.

The usher explained the codes on the curtains. A cross meant a woman; an arrow meant a man, and the symbols appeared in various combinations. Most were man and woman. The first booth he sampled had shown a slideshow of a woman and a man undressing, kissing and fondling each other and then performing the previously mysterious act. The basics of mammalian reproduction were not mystery to a country boy, but he had never seen humans doing it. Pedro watched it through twice, feeling nothing but mild curiosity.

The second booth had detailed drawings of naked women in various poses, legs spread and crotches on full display. Some were cupping their breasts as if offering fresh fruit at a stall, others sat with open mouths and tongues darting out to wet their lips, others were fingering themselves. Pedro skimmed through the selection and shrugged his shoulders. Why would anyone pay to see this?

The third booth had two arrows on it. Pedro licked his suddenly dry lips and swallowed hard before going in. The slides showed two naked men sitting side by side. They kissed in one slide. One licked the other's nipples in the next. Then their hands dropped and in a series of photos each stroked the other to climax. Pedro felt hot. A pulse pounded in his temple and he realized his own peck was getting hard, pushing against his pants. He suppressed the desire to unbutton and touch it. He stumbled out of the booth, almost running into another customer waiting a turn.

He spent the next couple of hours working his way through the room, viewing the contents of every booth that had two, or more, male symbols on it. He also checked out a few with two female signs, but neither the naked bodies of the women nor their sexual posturing interested him. Nor did a determined viewing of two more booths displaying sex between mixed couples.

By the end of his explorations he had seen samples of everything that Brother Matt had talked about. Men kissing and licking other men's pecks, men licking and fingering a partner's dark hole, men putting their pecks in another man's dark hole, and women who undressed to reveal male bodies under their skirts and frilly undergarments. He knew that he should have been disgusted. He should have gagged and turned away. He should have recognized everything he saw as loathsome and vile.

He sat in a coffee shop across the street, sipping a large coffee with a shot of rum; his aching balls making him wish he had yielded to the temptation to jerk his peck in one of the booths. He had to face the truth. He was one of the sinners the Warners had spoken of. He had never done any of the things he had seen, but he realized that he desperately wanted to. How could he take these desires back to Sweetwater? The pictures he had seen weren't going to fade from his memory. The desires he had felt since he started growing hair down there were not going to fade. One minute he felt sick inside, as if the doctor had told him he had some deadly disease. The next minute he felt relief. He wasn't alone. He might be a freak and a sinner, but he wasn't the only one. This was not a phase, like a kid wanting to run off and be a pirate or join the circus.

"So it looks like you found your way." A familiar figure slid onto the chair opposite him. Brother Matt, the Warner.

Pedro sat up straight and looked around as though he expected a posse to arrest and drag him off. "I came on the Peddler's Train with my dad's brandy. I was just curious. Please don't tell the folks at home."

"Relax." Brother Matt leaned forward. "You're not the first I've guided in. We Warners are not exactly what we seem." He tapped the green badge on his chest. "We work for the Sanctuary, helping people like you that are stuck in little towns with no knowledge of the outside world. I bet you thought you were the only boy who wanted to kiss your best friend. And you were miserable realizing that if you tried, or even said anything, that everyone would turn on you. You'd be a laughing stock, or you'd be prayed over at the Meeting, or maybe beat up by other boys, or even by your own kin.

"Maybe someone else in Sweetwater was wondering what it would be like to read some books that the Meeting Elders don't approve. Or another has questions about the writings of Elder Buckley. Maybe up in Allbekirk there was a girl that didn't want to marry and breed children until she dried up or died. Maybe in another little town there was someone who remembered hearing that the Natives around here had plants that showed the world as a different place. That's what we Warners do, plant a seed of hope that there is a place for the people born different or for the people who just want to *be* different."

Pedro stared at him. "You think someone like me is born this way?"

"How else? You certainly didn't learn it from anyone in Sweetwater." Brother Matt looked shrewdly at Pedro. "Did you?"

"No sir. I know Mr. Evans, the smith, gets kidded for never being married. But he just says his mother was so hard on his dad that he never wanted to let a woman have a chance at him." Pedro took another swallow of his coffee drink. "I've overheard some of the older men, ones that aren't Meeting members, joke with him. But they'd joke about not leaving him alone with a nice looking mare. And he'd joke right back that he preferred a cute little ass, and then wink and nod at an old picture of a lady riding a donkey that he had on the wall." Pedro blushed. "I never heard anyone joke that he might want to kiss men instead. Of course he's big enough to punch you into the next settlement if you riled him up, so maybe folks were afraid to say anything."

"Well, in a small place like Sweetwater there would have been jokes and rumors if he was interested in men. Not in front of him maybe, but I bet fathers would be careful about sending their sons over with a horse to shoe, if there was any talk. Just like careful mothers don't send their girls to the general store alone if the owner has a reputation for lewd behavior to women," replied Matt.

"The other boys; they'd always talk about this girl and that. How pretty they were. How it would feel to run your fingers through their long hair. How they had nice hips 'for bearing babies' and they'd wink and laugh and nudge each other. I would pretend to feel the same, laugh with them, remark on some girl's nice skin, or cup my hands against my chest and say that such a one was 'filling out nice.'" He shook his head. "I didn't care. They could have skin like buttermilk, hair to their bottom sides, bosoms like the biggest peaches my dad could grow, I didn't care.

"I'd be looking at my friend Benjamin, thinking how I'd like to run my fingers down the side of his face where his beard was just coming in. Or we'd all go swimming and I had to act extra crazy and rowdy to keep from thinking about what was inside the other boy's wet britches."

Brother Matt said, "I saw you go into the See Sin Shop. I guess you spent enough time to see what you needed."

"Yeah. But what do I do now? I can't just go back to Sweetwater and pretend to be like everybody else. Even if I married a girl I'm not sure I could do what's needed. I mean those pictures of men and women together . . ." He half gestured at his crotch. "Nothing.

"But my dad is counting on me to bring back the money from the brandy we sold and the supplies he ordered. If it was something decent that I wanted to stay for, like Benjamin going to the university . . . but I can't write and say I'm staying at the Sanctuary. Aunt Alice would never hold her head up in Meeting again."

"You're only fifteen, right?"

Pedro nodded.

Brother Matt put his hand over Pedro's. "Keep your word to your folks. Go back now. Keep quiet about what you've found out about yourself and about us Warners. Any money you get for chores, or hiring out during slow times on your dad's farm, getting a job in town: save it. In three years you can come back, a legal man. Finx Sanctuary will take you in. We have training for the kinds of jobs we need here. Or, better still: learn everything you can from your father about making spirits. A good distiller will always find work."

"Three years feels like forever."

"Remember, your friends aren't old enough to court the girls they talk about, not without a father, uncle or older brother chasing them off with a stick. If any of them got caught with a girl, doing the things they think about, they'd get whipped and sent to Reformatory. And their folks would be angry as heck about having to pay the costs. So you aren't really any worse off than them. They're doing what young men do for relief and so can you. No one else will know that you aren't thinking about bosoms and nice hips while you're doing it."

"No I guess not. From the way the older men looked sheepish when you talked about jerking your peck I guess everyone does it, even if it is a sin, and they all pretend no one knows."

"Now you're catching on. There is a lot of pretending goes on in the world. But I need to go now."

"Can I ask one more thing?" Pedro blurted out. "Are you like me? No offense, I just wondered why you would help me like this."

Brother Matt shook his head slowly. "No, I'm not interested in men that way. I'm more interested in getting people to challenge the politics and the power of the Meeting. Reading forbidden books and talking about ideas are what excite me. But the people who founded Sanctuary figured that if every persecuted group fought alone they would lose. Only by joining together can we protect each other. So the Elgeebeetas, the political radicals, the people in the entheogen movement and some of the religions that are called heresy by the Catholics and by the Meetings banded together. First they just hid out in remote areas. But the group over by Lost Angels got the idea of the Sanctuary and persuaded the war lord that held that territory before the Third Public retook it that it was an idea to benefit both sides.

"And when it worked out there, the idea spread to other areas. Sanctuaries provide certain services, like the See Sin shop, and actual whorehouses, drug dens and so forth. We make good money that way and pay whoever rules in the area—here it's the Local council—to leave us alone. They cooperate because they think it's useful to keep all the 'sin' in one place. You'll learn more when you come back."

"Thanks. Three years." Pedro nodded to himself. "Well, three years of waiting still seems like a long time, but I know Dad will be keeping me busy." He stood and shook Matthew Long's hand before heading for the gate.

Benjamin waited at the gate. From his flushed skin and slightly slurred speech Pedro guessed that he had been drinking more than he was used to. There was no age rule on drinking back in Sweetwater, but boys were usually restricted to wine or beer, or fruit ciders. Distilled liquor was for special occasions.

As they walked back to the stockade camp Benjamin shook his head ruefully. "Man, I'm sure glad I had the sense not to bring all my money with me. I would have spent too much for sure."

"Is drink that expensive here? I got a shot of rum in my coffee for only a quarter. I think the coffee itself actually cost more. Not sure why. People talk about real coffee, but without a glop of honey and some milk it tastes bitter as heck."

"No, it wasn't all on drink." Benjamin looked even more crestfallen. "Swear you won't tell anyone."

"Of course not. I spent my time in the See Sin shop and then in the coffee place. I looked at all kinds of pictures, even some moving pictures, of people doing it. Even some of the disgusting stuff the Warners talked about. You don't tell I did that, I won't tell on you."

"Well, I found an actual whore house. I didn't realize it at first. It just seemed like a drinking place with a bunch of pretty women sitting around in short dresses with not much over their bosoms. But then one caught me looking at her and came over and sat on my lap." He sighed deeply. "You can guess what happened then. So she reached down and sort of patted the front of my pants and said, 'Why don't we go upstairs and take care of this?'

"Oh man, the things she did. I thought I was going to die, it felt so good. I was with her an hour and we did it three times. Well the first time doesn't count 'cause I hardly got near her before—you know? I ended up spending five whole dollars.

"I'm going to have to stay away from this place or my money will be gone before I even start at the university."

Pedro thought about visiting the Sanctuary again before it was time for the Train to leave, but he knew the more time he spent there the harder it would be to go home. The trip back was quiet. He learned he could save on transport by renting and wrangling his own mules for the supplies he had purchased. His dad was duly impressed when he got back and gave him a third of the money he had saved. "You earned it; using your head.

"I've got a surprise for you. I've been courting the Widow Cassidy and she's agreed to have me."

"Benjamin's mom? That's great. He'll be glad to know his mom is taken care of while he's away. But what will happen to Aunt Alice?"

"She says she wants to move into town. The farm work is getting hard on her. That's one reason I thought of courting. But the settlement is growing and she thinks she can earn a living making cordials and herbal liqueurs. I'll supply her with the spirits for the base and she'll keep up her garden here." Andrew squeezed Pedro's shoulder. "You're a good man for worrying about her. But you know I would never let my sister want, especially after all she's done for us."

A few weeks after he got home Pedro received a letter from Benjamin. Ben had passed his exams with flying colors and started on his university courses. They were hard, the letter said, but he could already see what a difference the training would make to his future practice. "P.S.," he wrote, "I don't have to worry about spending too much money in town, like I talked about before you left. We students wear a uniform and certain places don't allow us in, by agreement with the university."

The following year Pedro asked his father if he could travel to Allbekirk to learn about making agave spirits. "I think I'd rather be a full time brewer and spirit maker than a farmer," he told Andrew. His father agreed that new skills were worth learning. "Cecily has a nephew who can help out on the farm if need be."

‡‡

Two years later Pedro prepared to escort another shipment of peach brandy to Finx. He also carried a selection of Aunt Alice's cordials. "I'll send the supplies and the payment back insured. But I'm going to stay in Finx a while and learn some more about distilling. I wrote to get information about that master distiller apprenticeship offered by the Guild."

It wasn't a lie, he told himself. He just hadn't mentioned that the Distiller's Guild was based in the Sanctuary. He was a man now, and it was time to live his own life. Dad had a new son with Cecily, and another child on the way. Aunt Alice would be disappointed, but he would have to live with his decisions long after she had gone to rest.

It was time to retrace the road to Finx.

The Last Farang

by Damian Macrae

farang

verb

1. Thai word for white people or Westerners, generally used in a non-derogatory connotation.

Example: Of course, drinks are expensive here, it caters mostly to farang.

Straits of Malacca, Siam and the Andaman Sea

In which our correspondent recounts his travels through the New Orient

> ****************************
> Aurora Shipping announces LAUNCH of the MV Southern Pointer
> 6500 tonne steel clipper, logged over 15knts in sea trials!
> Special launch rates apply for new FREIGHT consignments
> ** contact your agent today **
> FORGET waiting for that lottery win so you can FLY.
> Don't RISK your health to a smelly STEAMER
> Book your next trip on the MV Southern Pointer
> Luxury supernumerary cabins, standard berths
> and working passages available
> Aurora Shipping accepts
> all genuine UNCC subsidised migration vouchers
> ****************************

14th July, Singapore Harbour Locks

Spare a thought for your grandparents. Their stories of being whisked around the globe for an annual holiday sounds, like so much from that time, unbelievably extravagant. The convenient lack of hard copy photos or even letters gives the misty- eyed retellings a fantastical feel. Is Pop losing it for real, you think to yourself as he explains what a gap year entails. Your humble correspondent, just old enough to remember those days can inform you those stories are indeed true. My parents, who had travelled extensively by air in their youth, scrimped and saved for years to take my sister and I on a two week holiday to what was then called Thailand. I was eight years old, and it was the first and only time I travelled by aeroplane. It was an overnight flight, and I still remember staring through the window at the twinkling lights of fishing boats underneath us, whilst behind me, the darkened cabin was full of ephemeral faces, reflected from a hundred flickering blue screens.

But most of all, I remember the people. People in cars on the way to the airport. People in line, shuffling through military checkpoints with shoes off, emptying bags under the bored gaze of an immigration official. People sitting in front and behind me on the aeroplane, so close that even my tiny eight-year-old legs felt constrained. Sixty years later, as I stand in the forecastle of this fine vessel, watching the steamy coastline of Java gliding past, I remember that time. And I wonder what sort of society can take something so amazing and special as a trip across the world and turn it into a stressful ordeal.

They say it is not the destination, but the journey. I have taken passage on the *MV Timbercoast*, a steel-hulled, schooner-rigged cargo vessel that runs cargo and passengers between ports on the Malay Peninsula, West Siam, and Ceylon. My agent assures me the *MV Timbercoast* is a sturdy vessel with well-appointed and comfortable cabins. In my bag, carefully protected in a plastic laminate, I have a photo from those old times. It is of my family, standing in front of a large Buddha statue on top of a limestone karst peak. Buddha is sitting cross-legged and staring serenely into the distance. My parents are smiling as they grip my sister's and my shoulders to keep us looking at the camera. It is the only photo I have from back then, and I plan to revisit it and maybe find out if there is truly a difference between the journey and destination.

16th July, 25nm SW of Malay Peninsula

The Captain has been anxiously pacing all morning. The gentle breeze and calm seas, so welcome to this traveller of leisure, are a costly luxury for a working ship like the *Timbercoast*. In Singapore, the crew was open and friendly. Loud jests, friendly insults, and cocky banter thrown back and forth across the deck and amongst the rigging. After two days of wallowing in this feeble breeze, the crew is on edge and constantly casting furtive glances towards the steely-eyed Captain, ready to trim a sail or haul on a rope at an instant. No one wants to be held responsible if a moment is lost. I attempt light conversation and brevity with the crew, but after an ill-advised comment with the stout fellow manning the wheel, I quickly retire to my cabin lest another ill-advised remark cause me further grief. Travelling tip for my readers: do not cast any aspersions towards the appearance of a sailing vessel with its crew!

17th July, Dawn, Malacca Straits

Disaster averted, we are saved!

Hours sweltering in my tiny cabin had failed to yield any sleep so I stumbled outside to take some air. It was late, with no moon, and dark. The only noise was a low murmuring from a group of sailors sitting around a lantern playing a game of chance under the forward mainmast. After a few moments, when my senses had adjusted, I could make out shadows in the rigging and hear the occasional creaks and groans as the *Timbercoast* struggled to make steerage way. Occasionally a shadow would move, pulling on a rope or line, making minor adjustments to harvest every last breath of wind. Cautious, lest I provoke a harsh rebuke—or worse, a request to assist with some tedious nautical task—I crept to the stern and watched the ship's mediocre wake bubble and froth behind us.

Time passed—I am not sure how long. A faint breeze bought welcome relief from the cramped and hot cabin. The constant bubbling beneath me, signifying at least some progress, was relaxing. At some point, I realised I was not alone. Sitting a few metres distant, back against the stern rail, was a crew member, apparently asleep. Glancing around, I wondered at the sudden improvement of my night vision. The parsimonious Captain elected to not switch the rigging lights on this night and yet I could now see as if the moon was present. Looking back, I saw that the ship's wake was now glowing green and stretched out behind us into the darkness. I imagined looking from above and seeing our phosphorene trace cutting through the dark ocean.

The gentle tinkling of a nearby bell broke my reveries as I stared at our luminous wake. It was coming from near the sleeping crew member. Close examination revealed a fishing line ingeniously tied up to a small bell. I tried rousing the owner, but she rolled over and continued snoring. Unfazed by this setback, I began to pull the line, hand over hand, myself. I could feel the shudders and jolts through the line as the creature attempted escape. I must have shouted in excitement as I was soon surrounded by excited crew, all of them eagerly offering advice, many in languages I didn't recognise. I understood none of them, but together the excited babble required no translation. *Land that fish!* I redoubled my efforts, hauling on the thin line when I felt the beast's strength flag, paying it out when it wanted to run deep. Slowly, I brought it closer. A call of excitement rose from the crowd as a silvery shape flickered in and out of the luminous wake. The sight of my prey unlocked new reserves of strength and I hauled it to the surface, just above the rudder. It was white with blue stripes and at least the size of a dog. We would eat well tonight! A crew member was carefully lowered over the railing in a sling, intending to hook the fish with a cruel looking spike and haul it on deck. Another shout from behind me, this time clear and in English.

"LOOK OUT!"

I watched in horror as a vast shadow cut across the wake and engulfed the fish in a single bite before disappearing into the depths. The attack lasted less than a second, but I will always remember the look of terror in the crew member's eyes, his feet just inches from the surface.

They dragged him back on deck, his skin pale and hands shaking. The excited shouts stopped, replaced with an awe-struck silence. Then the Captain appeared, holding a mug of the foul liquor they always drank. He spoke for a minute, pointing at me, the distant horizon, and the shaken crew member. Then he laughed, slapped the kid on his back, handed him the mug and walked off. Somehow, I also found a drink in my hand. Everyone started hollering and laughing, each taking turns to retell this unusual event. Eventually the crew drifted back to wherever they came. The kid now had a smile on his face and wandered back to the forecastle to try his luck again. I stopped the stout wheelman, whom I knew spoke a little English, and asked him why everyone was so happy again. He said the Captain believes our sighting of such a rare, large fish was a good omen. Furthermore, our sacrifice of such a rare beast to the leviathan would be rewarded by the sea. The Captain also pointed out that maybe this strange white man might not be a Jonah after all and before the sun rises perhaps we will have our trade winds again. Sure enough, as the first faint rays of daybreak broke through the haze, I could see on the horizon towering thunderheads illuminated by the flicker of lightning. The monsoon had arrived, and with it the wind we needed to make a speedy (and profitable) journey.

Several hours later, the rigging hums and the *Timbercoast* is heeled over on a larboard tack. The crew darts about with an energised purpose, their on-time bonuses saved. I have been accorded a new level of respect: the victuals this morning were of a decidedly improved nature. I have become something of a minor celebrity, always being dragged about ship by a smiling crew member, happily explaining some deeply complex nautical contraption to the slow-witted, strange white man. Eventually, I manage to retire to my cabin. I intend to get some well-earned sleep before the afternoon heat makes the cabin unbearable.

‡‡

July 18th, Somewhere in the Malacca Straits

Today we bade farewell to the comforting sight of land. Up until now North Sumatra had always been there, a dirty smudge of green on our port horizon, reassuring if not beautiful. The continued favourable winds are "barrelling us up the strait," as Moko, the *MV Timbercoast* coxswain and apparently my new best friend, likes to say. This morning the straits finally opened and the sight of land disappeared into the hazy horizon. The Andaman Sea beckons!

July 20th, 73nm SW of Langkawi

We have all seen a ghost. Or, at least that is how the crew are acting after last night's events, and I confess to also feeling a little unsettled. It all began a little after midnight, well after the moon had set. Several of us were at the stern, trying our luck at fishing again. As usual, the Captain elected to not turn on the running lights and the *MV Timbercoast* glided through the gentle swell, guided by compass and starlight. I cannot say I agree with the Captain's choice to keep the ship dark. Who is to say we won't collide with another similarly parsimonious Captain? He did at least always insist on keeping a full watch during the night and it was a garbled shout from one of those dutiful souls in the crow's nest which first alerted us to the strange vessel.

"Hull up, three points to starboard!"

Down on deck we could not see the vessel yet, but a slight glow could be made out on the horizon. The Captain, looking uncharacteristically nervous, climbed the rigging to get a better look. A few minutes later he returned, his face displaying a mixture of fear and disbelief. Before the others could see, he composed himself, displaying the more normal look of stern disapproval. He whispered orders to Moko, who stood aside to allow the Captain to take the wheel himself. Ropes were hauled and sails trimmed in the true nautical tradition and I felt the *Timbercoast* heel a little more and the wake behind us bubbled a little more voraciously.

It wasn't long before the mystery vessel revealed itself. The orange glow on the horizon focused into an enormous steel ship, far larger than the *Timbercoast*, or even one of the new windjammers. It looked like our course would bring us close, maybe even within range of the powerful lights that that festooned the surface of that strange leviathan. As we drew even closer I could make out more details. It resembled one of the old merchant oil tankers, but had no smokestack. The massive hulk was a patchwork of hasty repairs and rusty steel plates, but here and there I could see remnants of the original colour, red. I now understood the Captain's concern: this ship was once part of the Great Red Fleet!

Alongside the cursed vessel, a collection of smaller vessels were tied up, including a modest sized schooner similar to the *Timbercoast*. I could see no flags or identification marks on any of them. Closer, and we could now make out crew on the leviathan and smaller vessels, running about, hauling ropes and moving cargo. We were so close it seemed impossible no one would notice us. Yet somehow, miraculously, we skirted the edge of their lights, dancing in and out of the shadows without incident, and carried on into the night. The Captain stayed at the wheel for another hour, until the last remnants of that ghastly glow disappeared under the stern rail.

It wasn't until well after breakfast the next day that I was able to speak to the Captain. I asked about the radiation danger. It was obvious he had not slept, but he took me back to his cabin and opened a locker under his bed. Inside was a small metal box, a analog numerical counter the only point of interest. Every few seconds it clicked as the Captain explained in broken English how he used to serve on a ship just like the one we passed. This was before the Hainan incident and the Amsterdam hijacking, back when ships of the Great Red Fleet were welcomed and celebrated in ports around the world. Before the rumours began of high crew turnover, dumping reactors at sea to avoid meltdowns, and the crippling construction and maintenance costs. Initial plans called for a fleet of one hundred vessels. They would travel the world's oceans, delivering Chinese goods to consumers and bringing back the raw resources the hungry factories required. The nuclear reactors never needed refuelling, precious oil could be saved for cars and air travel. As problems and costs mounted this was downsized to twenty. Then ten. After the Hainan incident and the irradiation of greater Hanoi, most ports with functioning governments banned their entry. The Captain resigned his commission not long after, taking the Geiger counter as a sort of severance package. The Captain says he is a lucky one; many of his former crewmates are dead now. Sail is much better, although he admitted an engine would have been useful last night. Wind and current forced him close. Thankfully the Geiger counter recorded nothing. I asked him if it still worked. The Captain shrugged with a look that seemed to say it made no difference either way now.

July 21st, Somewhere in the Andaman Sea

The mood was sombre the next morning. Running a sailing ship normally requires an excess of shouting, ringing bells, and the constant stampeding of an enthusiastic crew back and forth across the deck. But today the crew was subdued, performing their duties with a minimum of fuss. However, I must already be a salty sea dog as instead of using this quiet to advantage and getting some well-deserved sleep, I lay awake, my body already missing now familiar noises of sea travel. I rose at dawn and roamed the deck, talking with my ship mates about our brush with almost certain death the night before. I even tried my hand at fishing again, yet succeeded in catching nothing but the ubiquitous jellyfish.

As the day wore on, the Captain raised more sail and the mood lightened. I would like to think it was my philosophical conversation or witty banter that raised everyone's spirits. But on reflection I think it is the journey itself that cleared our minds. Hour after hour of clear, deep water sailing. Blue sky merging seamlessly into the ocean at the horizon. Wind blowing clean and fresh across the deck, the ship heeled just ever so slightly, and everyone's troubles and worries bubbling away into the frothy wake behind us. Moko says I overthink things, that everyone is happy because the Captain announced we were ahead of schedule and will overnight at Koh Phidon.

July 22nd, Dusk, Koh Phidon Floating Village

After two days of glorious blue water sailing, we glided into Koh Phidon anchorage at dusk. Decades ago Koh Phidon used to be a global tourist hotspot, the small island actually consisting of two separate limestone peaks, Doi Don on the east and Doi Tonsai to the west, joined in the middle by a narrow strand of sand covered in resorts, hostels, restaurants and bars. As the ocean rose, the town came with it, building up to avoid the waves. As it got deeper, only the richest could afford a secure footing, and a confusing jumble of old boats, floating piers, and bamboo bridges began to coalesce around the more permanent structures. Today, the central spit of sand is covered by at least twenty meters of water, yet the two peaks remain connected by the floating village. On the taller peak, Doi Don, sits a spectacular and exclusive resort catering to those rich enough to reach the island by air. On the other side, Doi Tonsai holds the various square, utilitarian storage units, power generation, and water filtration facilities, along with a small airfield for the launch and retrieval of guest helicopters and airships.

As the Captain fussed over the anchor placement for the *Timbercoast*, I took in the island. Tonight the resort looked busy. Hundreds of warm orange lights glowed between thick vegetation, and on the summit, bright, colourful lights strobed in time with a deep beat that could be heard across the bay. I could see three airships tethered at the airfield and as the crew began to lower our launch the distinctive heavy thump of an approaching helicopter announced the arrival of someone with riches beyond the imagination of anyone below in the village. The floating village was home to staff for the resort, the occasional fisherman, drug runners, gambling houses, brothels, and suppliers of all manners of illicit goods. The wealthy guests often visit the floating bazaar, considering it almost an attraction in itself and a chance to experience a gritty adventure with minimal risk. Keen operators who can match the ever-changing tastes of the fickle visitor can and do make substantial profits. Which is why, even after monsoonal storms sometimes sweep away the entire village, it is quickly rebuilt.

The crew have drawn straws to determine who remains behind for first watch. There is some discussion to decide if the first or last watch is preferable but no one volunteers to go first. Moko beams at me; he has avoided any duties for tonight. As we begin rowing towards the ramshackle shore, fireworks are launched from Doi Don and the bay becomes alight with ripples of purple, red and green.

July 24th, Krabi Harbour

The journey from Koh Phidon to Krabi was uneventful, at least as far as I can recall. How the crew managed to effectively function after such a night I will never understand, but it seems to be a skill that all mariners possess. We ghosted into Krabi Harbour on a fading afternoon breeze, passing over the sunken ruins of old Krabi and anchored two hundred meters from the recently constructed wharf. A steamer, two coastal luggers and a windjammer were already alongside, men and cranes hauling crates and barrels onto the waiting trams. On the northeast side, in front of mangroves and coconut palms, the harbour was shallow. The beached remains of rusted container ships fought for space between the skeletal ruins of old Krabi, some of the twisted rebar and steel poking above the water at low tide. Overlooking it all, on top of a tall narrow karst peak, was the Buddha, the setting sun reflecting golden light from his serene face. The Captain seemed to think we would be at least a day and I should have plenty of time to ascend the eight hundred steps in the morning so I retired to my cabin early and fell asleep to the sound of harbour gulls and longshoremen curses.

Early the next morning, with a small dinghy personally loaned to me from the Captain, I found myself rowing towards the base of the karst mountain. I picked my way down channels between the dead ships, but the water was murky and it was sometimes difficult to make out the concrete reefs of the old city ruins. I gingerly picked my way through, taking care not to scratch or damage the Captain's personal dinghy. Finally, I pulled the dinghy up onto a small sandy beach, dense mangroves hemmed in on both sides with a small path leading towards concrete stairs. A troupe of monkeys watched me from a tree, and looking steep sides I could make out the distinctive orange robes of two monks making the ascent. I placed my feet on the first step, faded paint announcing it was number 379, quietly thanked the rising seas for making this easier, and eagerly began the climb, keen to set a good pace and maybe even catch the leisurely monks.

Within a hundred steps I had to stop, the sweat already thick on my skin and running down my arms and back. The heavy, humid air refused to absorb any more moisture. Wiping my face with a small towel, I looked back across the harbour. In the distance, I could see the Captain and Moko on the *Timbercoast* poop deck, gently guiding the ship towards the wharf. Below me, the unappealing murky green water was not enhanced by the rusting hulks or twisted ruins that resided within. A crash of branches above revealed the monkeys had followed me. Anxious to avoid their attentions, I resumed the climb at a more sedate pace, ignoring the chorus of mocking cries and hoots.

I passed the halfway mark, but several hundred steps still remained and my legs were like jelly. Sweat poured down my arms, beading in long drops at the tips of my fingers. The monkey troupe could be heard crashing through the treetops a little below me, so I took a chance to sit and rest. What little cooling I had from forward motion was removed and almost immediately a fresh burst of perspiration issued from my sodden skin, running down my forehead, back, and arms. I took a long draught from a water bottle, the tepid, slightly salty liquid still managing to be refreshing. From this height, the harbour looked a little cleaner, the murky green now a pale turquoise, and patches of blue sky breaking through the haze. At the outer channel marker, a small tug noisily belched black smoke as it nudged one of the coastal luggers into the main channel. Raising sails to catch the freshening breeze, the lugger heeled over and began pushing into the turgid swell under its own power. Occasionally the odd shout or cry from crew in the rigging drifted across the harbour. Presently she rounded the headland and disappeared from sight. The *Timbercoast* was now at the wharf and I could the see the crew already working at unloading cargo. Ignoring the protestations of my legs, I stood back up and continued up the stairs.

The worn paint announced the final step number as 1237. For some reason, no one had corrected the mistake, perhaps not wanting to tempt fate that the rising oceans were finished. I stood at the edge of a large concrete floor, covered in red tiles and surrounded by a freshly painted white concrete railing. A smaller raised platform on the left held a modest stupa, painted gold. To the right was a collection of smaller statues, the two monks quietly making offerings of incense and arranged flowers. They glanced back at me. I nodded in acknowledgement and they went back to their worship. In front of me, towering over everyone, was Buddha sitting cross-legged and staring over the harbour. He was over eight meters tall, the golden paint still gleaming in the morning sunlight. I thought back to my parent's photo; the buddha had a different coat of paint back then. Red clothes, pale skin, and black hair looking over old Krabi, the ocean safely on the horizon. And in the background of the photo, hordes of tourists milling about, recording everything with the ubiquitous screens. I glanced around. Besides the monks I was alone, and there was no one to photograph me. I thought about asking the monks to take the photo for me, but it felt wrong to interrupt them more than I already had. I thought about balancing the camera on the railing and using the timer function. The thought of such an expensive device falling, or more likely, getting pushed by the nearby monkeys, was not a pleasant one. Instead, I walked to the edge, held the railing and shared the view with Buddha. From up here the harbour gleamed, with none of the rubbish or pollution was evident. The sunken wrecks were blurred, their sharp edges already rusting away. In a few decades, there would be nothing left except an iron rich sand bar with scattered skeleton-like keels preserved in the mud beneath.

It is the journey not the destination which matters. I think today, in the world we live in, I understand this now. For my parents, journeys back then tended to be short, yet somehow tedious and spirit-sapping for all that. Cheap journeys means quick travel, rushing from one hotspot to another, locals crowding to earn their share from the economic heavyweights stumbling blindly through their country on a ten day cultural binge. The first leg of my journey has already taken longer than most complete holidays back then, and when I leave tomorrow on the morning tide I will have spent less time here then I did with my parents all those years ago. Yet, standing between Buddha and the blue harbour below, it doesn't seem to matter. I hurry back down the steps, the camera sitting unused in my bag. Ceylon awaits!

Don't miss a single issue of Into the Ruins

Already a subscriber? Your subscription may be expiring if you haven't recently renewed!

Renew Today

Visit intotheruins.com/renew
or send a check for $39 made out to Figuration Press to
the address below

Don't forget to include the name and address attached to your current subscription and to note that your check is for a renewal. Your subscription will be extended for four more issues.

Subscribe Today

Visit intotheruins.com/subscribe
or send a check made out to Figuration Press for $39 to:

Figuration Press
3515 SE Clinton Street
Portland, OR 97202

Don't forget to include your name and mailing address, as well as which issue you would like to start with.